CLAUDIA AND THE TERRIBLE TRUTH

Other books by
Ann M. Martin

Leo the Magnificat
Rachel Parker, Kindergarten Show-off
Eleven Kids, One Summer
Ma and Pa Dracula
Yours Turly, Shirley
Ten Kids, No Pets
Slam Book
Just a Summer Romance
Missing Since Monday
With You and Without You
Me and Katie (the Pest)
Stage Fright
Inside Out
Bummer Summer

THE KIDS IN MS. COLMAN'S CLASS series
BABY-SITTERS LITTLE SISTER series
THE BABY-SITTERS CLUB mysteries
THE BABY-SITTERS CLUB series
CALIFORNIA DIARIES series

CLAUDIA AND THE TERRIBLE TRUTH

Ann M. Martin

SCHOLASTIC INC.
New York Toronto London Auckland Sydney

Cover art by Hodges Soileau

ISBN 0-590-05995-5

12 11 10 9 8 7 6 5 4 3 2 1 8 9/9 0 1 2 3/0

Printed in the U.S.A. 40

First Scholastic printing, March 1998

The author gratefully acknowledges
Ellen Miles
for her help in
preparing this manuscript.

"Aah! Alone at last." We gazed deeply into each other's eyes and smiled happily. Then the object of my affections began to drool.

Was I grossed out? No way. I just wiped off the drool with the cuff of my shirt and went on gazing and smiling.

Now, if I were talking about a *guy* — say, my boyfriend, Josh — things might be different. I'd be pretty freaked if he started to drool in front of me. But a little drool is nothing between me and my beloved cousin, Lynn. She can do no wrong, as far as I'm concerned. And since she's only six months old and teething, her lack of saliva control is no big surprise.

"I can't believe you're mine, all mine, for a whole week," I told Lynn. She gurgled happily. She may not be able to talk yet, but I can translate her little noises. She was letting me know she was as excited as I was about our time together.

Five minutes earlier, Lynn's parents had finally left. My uncle Russ practically had to shove my aunt Peaches out the door. "What if she starts running a fever?" Peaches asked, clutching Lynn as if she couldn't bear to turn her over to me. "What if she falls out of her crib?"

"Claudia knows what to do," said my mother soothingly, putting an arm around Peaches. (They're sisters.) "She can handle any situation that comes up. Remember, she's a professional baby-sitter."

I nodded. "That's right," I said. "Lynn will be in the care of a full-fledged founding member of the BSC." I grinned proudly. I didn't have to explain to Peaches and Russ about the BSC. They know those initials stand for Baby-sitters Club, and they know what the club is all about. You can't find better, more experienced sitters anywhere.

"Not to mention the BSC member's sibling and parents," added my older sister, Janine. "We'll be here too."

"And you two deserve some time off," put in my dad. "After all, you haven't had a vacation since Lynn was born."

"Hear, hear," said Russ. "Now, let's say good-bye and be on our way. There's a golf ball with my name on it, and a nice hot sauna waiting for you." They'd booked a week at a classy resort about an hour and a half away. Russ pretended to swing a golf club. It was the first day of March, so he wouldn't be doing a lot of outdoor golfing. But the place had an indoor driving range, and Russ couldn't wait to check it out.

Reluctantly, Peaches handed Lynn over to me. "Don't forget to warm her formula," she said. "But don't make it too hot. She might — "

" — burn her mouth," I said, nodding as I hugged Lynn to my chest. "I know." Peaches had given us a five-page memo detailing Lynn's routines. Not that I needed it. I've taken care of Lynn plenty of times — she's practically spent as much time at my house as she has at her parents'! But just to make Peaches feel comfortable, I recited her directions from page three, paragraph seven: "Warm the formula until a few drops shaken on the inside of your wrist feel neither hot nor cold. Hold Lynn in a near-upright position for feeding. Make sure to burp her afterward." I could have continued, with the three paragraphs specifying exactly *how* to burp her, but it didn't seem necessary. Peaches was nodding.

"I guess she'll be okay," she said. "After all, this is like her second home." She gave Lynn one last kiss, turned to join Russ, and, without looking back, managed to walk out the door. I knew that had required a humongous effort on her part, so I took pity on her. I followed them to the door and said in a squeaky voice, "Bye-bye, Mama, bye-bye, Dada! Have a good time!" I lifted Lynn's arm and made her wave to them. Russ cracked up, and even Peaches managed a shaky smile. I knew they'd have a terrific time once the trauma of leaving Lynn was over. I stood in the doorway, waving to them until their car was out of sight. Then I carried Lynn straight up to my room, closed the door behind us, plopped her down on the bed, and lay down next to her.

I'd been waiting for this moment all day: the moment when I would have Lynn to myself.

Speaking of "myself," I guess I should tell you who I am. My name's Claudia, as you have already guessed. Claudia Lynn (yes, that's where the baby's name came from) Kishi. I'm thirteen years old and I live in Stoneybrook, Connecticut, with my mom, my dad, and Janine, who's sixteen. All of us are Japanese-American. Janine is a genius. My mom's a librarian (she'd left her job early that day in order to be home when Lynn arrived), and my dad does something I'll never understand with stocks and bonds. My mother's mother, Mimi, lived with us until she died not long ago. I was closer to Mimi than to anyone else in my family, and I miss her every single day. I wish she'd lived long enough to meet Lynn.

Even though Lynn is only half Asian (Uncle Russ is Irish, with red hair and freckles), I think she'll grow up to look like her mom. She already has dark hair and dark, almond-shaped eyes. Maybe a freckle or two will pop out one day, just to make Russ feel better.

And if I have anything to say about it, she'll be the most creatively dressed kid in Stoneybrook, thanks to her cousin Claud. I may not be a genius like Janine (I'm not even close, since she's taking college courses while she's in high school and I just spent some time repeating seventh grade), but if there's one thing I am good at, it's dressing with style and flair. Actually, I don't mean to sound egotistical, but I guess I'm pretty creative overall. I love to paint and draw and sculpt. In fact, I look at life in artistic terms. My room is full of projects in every stage, from just started to finished-but-could-still-be-improved-upon. And my outfits are one-of-a-kind creations, featuring my own embroidery, tie-dyeing, jewelry making, etc. I try to fix my hair a different way every day. I even find creative ways to make chores like table setting and salad making fun.

However, I'm not so great at salad *eating*. I'd rather eat a Twinkie. I love junk food. It's sort of an obsession of mine. I keep an eye out for new products, but I also like the classics such as Doritos and Snickers bars. My parents have outlawed junk food in the Kishi home, but that doesn't stop me. I just hide what I buy, along with the Nancy Drew mysteries my mom thinks aren't "challenging" enough for me to be reading. (*Wrong*.)

I glanced at Lynn, who had apparently just discovered the fact that she has toes. She was thrilled. (Babies are easily pleased.) I wondered when she'd be ready to forget the baby formula and move on to some *real* food, perhaps some Mallomars. Soon, I hope. And while she's eating them, I can read Nancy Drew mysteries to her. I can hardly wait.

I'm not worried about corrupting her. Good genes run in our family. Look at me. I'm perfectly healthy, with clear skin and a decent figure. You'd never know I'm the Junk Food Queen of Stoneybrook.

Lynn smiled up at me and I grinned back. Then I picked her up and gave her a squeeze. "I am so happy you're here, you little pumpkin," I said, rolling over to let her lie on my belly. She gurgled. "I know, I know," I said. "You're happy to *be* here, aren't you?" She's such a calm, happy baby. Instead of being freaked out by a change of pace, she enjoys it.

I guess I'm the same way. Things had been changing lately, and I thought it was exciting. The BSC had lost a pair of regular sitting charges: Corrie and Sean Addison. They'd moved away because Mrs. Addison was offered a better job in Seattle, and they'd sold their house to a new family, the Nichollses. The kids — two boys named Joey and Nate — seem nice. Joey's seven and Nate is just five. Their mom works at the library with my mom, and I'm not sure what their dad does. The time I met him, he seemed a little, I don't know, pushy or something. He kept bugging Joey and Nate about helping him organize the garage. I mean, they're just little kids, and they were doing their best, as far as I could see.

I wonder if they'll end up as BSC clients. If they do, they won't be our only new clients.

Lou McNally is an eight-year-old girl who once spent a few weeks living with some other clients of ours, as a foster child. At the time, we thought she was the "Worst Kid Ever." That's what Kristy called her. It turned out that she was just very unhappy. Her father had recently died and her mother had left the family years before. Eventually, she and her eleven-year-old brother, Jay, went to live with an uncle — their father's brother — and his wife. Now the McNallys have moved to Stoneybrook and Lou is doing much better. My friends and I have been sitting for her and Jay. We love having new clients.

Meanwhile, I'm going to concentrate on taking care of my incredibly adorable, totally lovable, majorly wonderful baby cousin.

"What should we do first?" I asked Lynn. "Play peekaboo? Change you into another one of your outfits? Teach you how to play This Little Piggy? Or just lie here and snuggle?"

Lynn didn't answer. Then I heard a tiny baby snore and realized she'd fallen asleep on my stomach.

"Oh," I said softly. "You want to take a nap. Sounds like an excellent idea." I closed my eyes and lay there happily, feeling the soft, warm weight of Lynn and smelling her delicious baby smell. She was trusting enough to fall asleep on top of me. Somehow, in her little baby mind, she knew she was perfectly safe with me. And I felt safe with her too. Like nothing could go wrong in a world with Lynn in it. It was a wonderful feeling, and I wanted it to last forever.

But before I could drift into the same kind of peaceful sleep Lynn was enjoying, I heard the thump of feet coming up the stairs. I rubbed my eyes, yawned, and tried to figure out how to sit up without waking Lynn. Those thumping feet told me that our BSC meeting was about to start.

The door to my room flew open and Kristy Thomas, the BSC's president, burst in. "Is she here — ?" she began loudly. Then she spotted Lynn, and her voice dropped to a whisper. "Oh, she's beautiful," Kristy said. "And she's grown so much already. I can't believe it." She reached out to stroke Lynn's head.

Lynn was stirring by then, making little baby noises as she stretched. "Can you go downstairs and ask my mom to heat some formula?" I whispered to Kristy. "I bet she'll be hungry when she wakes up."

Kristy nodded. "I'll bring it up in a couple of minutes," she promised. She was still gazing at Lynn.

Lynn stretched again. "Hurry!" I said. I didn't want Lynn to have to wait.

Kristy bolted out the door. I started cooing over Lynn, telling her softly that a snack was on its way.

By the time Kristy came back with a warm bottle of formula, the rest of the BSC members had arrived and Lynn, who was wide awake by then, was the center of attention. I'd promised everyone a turn at holding her, but I wanted to be the one to begin giving her the bottle. Kristy handed it over reluctantly and I offered it to Lynn. Her eyes closed in happy satisfaction as she sucked and drank, and my friends clustered around, discussing in whispers her shiny black hair, her perfect little hands, her gorgeous ears.

"Okay, I have two announcements," Kristy said finally. "First of all, I hereby call this meeting to order. And second, it's my turn." She sat down in the director's chair by my desk and held out her arms.

Carefully, I transferred Lynn and her bottle. It was hard to give her up, but she didn't seem to mind being held by another person. At first, that made me just the tiniest bit jealous, since I want her to love me best of all. But then I decided that it was a good character trait for my cousin to have. She makes friends easily and adjusts well to new surroundings. I hope she'll always be that way.

I wonder if the personality you have as a baby stays with you. My mom tells me that I started making finger paintings with my strained carrots and mashed peas. "An artist right from the beginning," she says. I looked around the room at my friends, trying to picture each of them as a baby. Had their infant personalities followed them as they grew?

I actually knew Kristy as a baby, since she and I lived across the street from each other back then. Of course, I don't remember what she was like, since I was a baby too. But I'd bet anything that Baby Kristy was headstrong and determined to have things her way. She probably had definite opinions and wasn't shy about sharing them.

Kristy (grown-up Kristy, that is) is the driving force behind the BSC. In fact, the business was originally her idea. Here's how it works: The club meets in my room, since I have my own phone, with a private line (that's why I'm the vice-president). We meet on Mondays, Wednesdays, and Fridays, from five-thirty until six, and parents call us during those times to set up sitting jobs. We're very organized. We keep a club record book with information on our clients and a calendar with our schedules. We also keep a club notebook, in which we each write up every single one of our jobs, which is *not* my favorite chore. Reading everybody else's entries helps us stay up-to-date on what's happening with the kids we sit for. The parents love that.

We're excellent sitters: responsible, punctual,

and caring. We love hanging out with our charges. We're not the kind of sitters who stick a movie into the VCR to keep the kids busy while we raid the fridge and talk on the phone. We think it's more fun to pull out our Kid-Kits (boxes we've filled with fun stuff such as stickers and markers and hand-me-down toys and books) and have a good time with our charges. You can imagine why kids — and parents — like us so much.

And it's all due to Kristy. She has a real talent for coming up with terrific ideas, and that headstrong nature of hers means she knows how to make sure her ideas are carried out. Some people might call her bossy, but that's just Kristy.

Kristy has brown hair and eyes and absolutely *zilch* in the way of fashion sense. Her closet is filled with jeans, turtlenecks, and running shoes. She has a huge family: her mom and stepdad, two older brothers and one younger one, a younger stepbrother and stepsister, a little adopted sister who's just learning to talk, and a grandmother who has more energy than all of the others put together. Plus a whole zoo's worth of pets. They all live very happily in her stepdad's mansion across town. Her stepfather's name, by the way, is Watson Brewer, and he happens to be a millionaire.

Kristy's life wasn't always so easy. In fact, it

was rough going for a long time, after her father left the family when she was six. I'd say she and her mom and brothers deserve some happiness.

"Um, Kristy?" Mary Anne Spier, Kristy's best friend, was holding out her arms. "Do you think I could have a turn?"

Kristy grumbled, but she knew she couldn't hog Lynn forever. She gave her to Mary Anne, who settled herself next to me on the bed. Mary Anne, who has brown hair and brown eyes just like Kristy, is the club's secretary. She keeps track of all our clients and monitors our schedules so well that she always knows at a glance who's free for what job.

Okay, let me think about Baby Mary Anne, whose mother died when Mary Anne was very, very young. She would have been quiet, that's for sure. And much more bashful than Lynn, but very sweet and loving.

After her mom died, Mary Anne lived with her grandparents for awhile. After that, she grew up with just her dad for family. Until recently, that is. Not long ago, her dad remarried a woman he'd gone out with in high school! (Sigh. So romantic. Mary Anne loves that kind of thing.) The woman had moved to California, married another man, and had two children. Then, when that marriage ended, she'd moved back to Stoneybrook, bringing her kids along.

One of them was Dawn Schafer, who became one of Mary Anne's best friends, and then her stepsister. Dawn also belonged to the BSC and served as our alternate officer, which meant she took over the duties of anyone who couldn't make it to a meeting. However, Dawn and her younger brother, Jeff, have both moved back to California to live with their dad. I know Mary Anne misses her sister a ton (we all do), but at least Dawn comes back to visit on some holidays and school vacations.

Mary Anne's not entirely lonely without Dawn, anyway. She still has Kristy, plus Tigger (her gray kitten) and Logan (her boyfriend) to keep her company.

As I was thinking about Mary Anne, the phone rang and she picked it up. "Hello, Baby-sitters Club," she said. She listened for a moment, then said she'd call right back. "That was Mrs. Nicholls," she reported after she'd hung up. "She needs a sitter for Monday afternoon." Mary Anne began to look in the record book to see who was free. It wasn't easy with Lynn on her lap.

"I'll take her," volunteered Abby Stevenson, who was sitting on the floor, leaning against my bed. She stood up and held out her arms for Lynn, and Mary Anne turned back to our schedules.

"Would you like the job, Claud?" Mary Anne

asked me. "It looks like you're the only one free that day."

"Sure," I said. "I've been wanting to get to know those kids better anyway."

Mary Anne called Mrs. Nicholls back and told her everything was set. Meanwhile, Abby was on the floor, making funny faces at Lynn, who was fascinated.

I don't know Abby very well, since she, her twin sister, Anna, and their mom moved here only recently. They used to live on Long Island, in New York. Their dad died in a car crash a few years ago.

But I know her well enough to guess that she was a happy, laughing baby. Abby is full of fun, though sometimes I think she's hiding a lot of sadness about her dad. She's full of energy too, even though she has asthma and is allergic to just about everything under the sun. Sneezes and wheezes or not, Abby is out there playing soccer, running, skiing, swimming, you name it. If it's athletic, Abby does it and does it well. Her sister's not much of an athlete, but she can play the violin like a pro. Anna puts all of her energy into music. In fact, she's so busy with rehearsals and all that she didn't join the BSC along with Abby, though we had invited them both to become members. (By the way, Abby is our alternate officer, now that Dawn has moved away.)

Abby and Anna both have curly dark hair and dark eyes. Sometimes they wear contacts, sometimes glasses. Anna found out recently that she has scoliosis, which is curvature of the spine, and even though it's not a bad case, she has to wear a brace for awhile.

"Okay, time's up," said Stacey McGill, who is the BSC's treasurer and also my best friend. "Hand that child over."

Abby laughed and made one more face at Lynn. Then she scooped her up and gave her to Stacey. "Oh, you are such a little snuggle-bumps," Stacey told Lynn. She turned to me. "She is so cute," she said. "How many outfits did your aunt bring over? Maybe we can change her later."

That's Stacey for you. She's even more obsessed with clothes than I am. I bet Baby Stacey was picking out her own rompers before she could even say "Mama." And since Baby Stacey lived in Manhattan, I bet her rompers were the height of fashion.

Stacey lives in Stoneybrook now, but she still visits Manhattan often, to see her dad. (Her parents are divorced.) And when she's in the Big Apple, Stacey stocks up on all the trendiest, most sophisticated clothes anyone in Stoneybrook has ever seen.

But there's a lot more to Stacey than good taste in clothes. She's a strong person who's had to deal with some tough circumstances in her life: not just the divorce but diabetes as well. As a diabetic, Stacey knows that her disease will probably be with her all her life but that she can control it if she's careful. You see, diabetes interferes with the way the body processes sugar. This means that Stacey has to be very careful about what she eats. Plus, she has to test her blood sugar and give herself insulin injections every day. I don't think I could do it, but Stacey says I would if I had to, just the way she does.

As treasurer of the club, Stacey collects dues every Monday. She keeps track of how much she collects, and we use the money to pay for such things as my phone bill and gas money for Kristy's brother, who drives Kristy and Abby to our meetings. Stacey actually *likes* math and is good at it, so she makes a perfect treasurer.

"What's that, Lynn?" Jessi Ramsey, who was sitting on the floor next to her best friend, Mallory Pike, cupped her hand around one ear as she leaned toward Stacey. "You want to come see me and Mal? Of course you can!" Grinning, she jumped up to take Lynn from Stacey. Then, gracefully, since she's a ballet dancer, she sank back to her spot near Mal.

"Peekaboo, I see you," Mal sang, hiding her eyes with her hands. She has *zillions* of younger brothers and sisters (okay, seven), so she's a pro at entertaining babies.

Jessi and Mal are our junior officers. The rest of us are thirteen and in the eighth grade. Jessi and Mal are eleven and in the sixth. They're just as responsible as we are, but they're only allowed to cover afternoon jobs, unless they're baby-sitting for their own families.

Jessi, who's African-American, lives with her younger sister, her baby brother, her aunt, and her parents. She loves ballet (I'm sure Baby Jessi was dancing around on tiptoes in her crib) and reading. Mal, who has reddish-brown hair and freckles, is a reader too. I bet she was always grabbing at books when she was a baby. She wants to write and illustrate children's stories someday.

Now you've met everyone in the BSC, except our two associate members, who usually don't come to meetings but who are always ready to help out if we're swamped with work. One of them is Shannon Kilbourne, who lives in Kristy and Abby's neighborhood. The other is Logan Bruno, Mary Anne's boyfriend. Both of them are terrific with kids.

As our meeting was ending that day, Kristy reminded us that St. Patrick's Day was coming up. "I hear there's going to be a parade downtown this year," she reported. "And I hear some of the kids want to march in it. Maybe we should help them build a float or teach them some kind of marching routine. Let's talk about it more at our next meeting."

I knew Kristy would probably have a plan by then. She loves sinking her teeth into something like that. (I, on the other hand, mostly like to sink my teeth into chocolate.)

The meeting ended, and my friends took off, leaving me alone again with Lynn. "What did you think of our meeting?" I asked her. "Maybe someday you can be in a club." She smiled at me and gurgled. "Oh, you want to be president, do you? Fine by me, Miss Lynn." I lay back on my bed again with her on my stomach. We were alone once more and I couldn't have been happier.

"Hi, I'm — " I wasn't sure if he would remember me.

"Claudia!" Mr. Nicholls finished. "Sure, come on in." He made a welcoming gesture and held the door open for me.

I was surprised that Mr. Nicholls remembered my name. We'd only met before for about two seconds. Not only that, but since he was new in the neighborhood he must have met dozens of people recently. I was impressed.

It was Monday afternoon, and I was arriving for my job with the Nicholls boys. I'd had a hard time giving up any of my precious hours with Lynn, but I was excited about getting to know our new clients.

Mr. Nicholls was wearing a very nice-looking dark blue suit. He's short with close-cropped brown hair and a sandy mustache.

Somehow I had been expecting Mrs. Nicholls

to answer the door, but now that I thought about it, I knew she probably wouldn't be home until later. My mom doesn't get home until after six, but a lot of the librarians leave at five.

Mr. Nicholls checked his watch. "I'd better be on my way," he told me. "Boys!" he called out.

Nate and Joey came running down the stairs. I gave them a little wave hello as their dad began to talk to them. "I'm going out now," he said, "and Claudia will be your baby-sitter. I want you two to behave. If you don't, Claudia will let me know. Do you understand?"

"Yes," said Joey in a small voice.

Nate just nodded.

"What's that?" asked their dad, cupping his ear. "I don't think I heard you."

"YES," the boys said together.

"That's better." Mr. Nicholls smiled at me. "I'll be back in a couple of hours. Help yourself to a snack," he said, dropping the stern voice he'd been using with his sons. "The boys may have one cookie each, and they know the rules about where to eat them," he added, giving Nate a significant look. Nate dropped his eyes. Maybe he had a hard time remembering the rules, whatever they were.

Mr. Nicholls leaned toward the hall mirror to check his tie. Then he picked up his briefcase, said good-bye, and left. I suddenly realized I had no idea where he was going. Normally I'd have asked for an emergency phone number, especially with a new client. But I knew Mrs. Nicholls was at the library so I decided it didn't matter.

"I hope he's going to a job interview," muttered Joey as soon as his father's car had pulled out of the driveway.

"Joey!" said Nate. "Shhh. He'd be mad if he heard you say a bad thing like that."

What was so bad about it? I wasn't sure I understood. Then a light dawned. Maybe Mr. Nicholls was out of work and ashamed about it. I didn't think there was anything wrong with being out of work. Lots of people find themselves in that position. I remember when Mal's dad lost his job. But maybe Mr. Nicholls was sensitive.

"What kind of work does your dad do?" I asked Joey.

"He used to work for a computer company," Joey answered. He didn't seem to want to say any more about it than that. "Can we please have our snack now?" he asked.

"Sure," I said. "Cookies, here we come!"

"You better take your shoes off first," said Nate.

I raised my eyebrows.

"He's right," said Joey. "It's so we don't track in mud."

"But there's no mud — " I began. Then I stopped. If that was the house rule, it wasn't my business to question it. I untied my Pumas (totally hip '70s-type sneakers — very cool at SMS) and left them with the other shoes lined up in the front hall.

The kitchen was spotless. Four high-backed wooden chairs sat around a square wooden table, each chair pushed in perfectly straight. The counters were wiped clean, and canisters for coffee, tea, sugar, and flour were lined up like little soldiers. There wasn't a single dish in the gleaming sink, and I didn't see a single fingerprint on the door of the fridge. I looked around, amazed. I'd never seen a kitchen so tidy, especially in a house with two boys.

"Dad likes a clean kitchen," Joey explained, as if he'd read my mind. He pointed to a cabinet over the fridge. "The cookies are up there."

I opened the cabinet door to see a neatly arranged row of cereals, crackers, and cookies. I reached up and took out a bag of Chips Ahoy. Then I found a plate in another cabinet (do I have to mention how perfectly stacked the china was?) and put a few cookies onto it. "Milk?" I asked the boys.

They exchanged a look. "No, thanks," said Joey, speaking for both of them.

I shrugged. "Okay." I pulled out a chair and sat down. They did too. We each took a cookie, and the boys sat quietly, nibbling at theirs.

I studied the boys. Joey was thin, with dark brown hair. His eyes were big and green and worried-looking. He reminded me of some kind of shy animal, maybe a deer. Nate was chunkier, though he was still shorter than his older brother. He had big brown eyes, and brown hair with blond highlights, like his dad's. I remembered meeting Mrs. Nicholls at the library. She was a birdlike woman with chin-length blonde hair and green eyes.

I helped myself to another cookie and offered the plate to Joey and Nate. They shook their heads. "Oops," I said, remembering. "That's right. Your dad said one each." I shoved the plate aside.

The boys were a little shy, but they seemed friendly enough. Being new in town, maybe they needed a little help meeting people. Suddenly I had a great idea. "Hey, you know what?" I asked. "My friend Stacey is baby-sitting right next door, for Stephen Stanton-Cha. He hasn't lived here for very long. I bet he's thrilled to have you two for new neighbors."

"We met Stephen already," said Joey. "He's really nice. And he has tons of cool toys and stuff." For the first time, I saw his eyes really light up with interest.

"He's cool," agreed Nate.

"So, why don't we hang out over there for awhile?" I asked. "I know Stacey and Stephen would be glad to have us."

Nate looked excited. "Can we really go?" he asked.

"Sure, why not?" I answered.

"I don't know," said Joey, shaking his head. "We're not supposed to leave the house unless Mom or Dad is with us."

"Oh, right," said Nate. The excitement had gone out of his voice.

"But I'm the baby-sitter," I said. "And I would be going with you." Joey looked unsure.

"It's okay, really," I promised. "I've taken care of plenty of kids, and none of their parents ever minded if I took them to play with other kids, as long as we were home on time."

"Let's go, Joey. Please?" begged Nate.

"I'll leave a note for your parents," I said. "We always do that anyway. Your mom will probably be home at a little after five. I don't know when your dad's coming home, but it won't be for awhile."

My reassurances must have worked, because finally Joey agreed. "Okay, but we're not going to stay too long," he said.

"Great," I said, jumping up to give Stacey a call. "I'll just make sure they're around." As I headed for the phone on the wall I noticed Joey and Nate standing up and pushing their chairs in carefully. Nate even pushed mine in, making sure the placement was exactly right. And Joey rinsed off the plate we'd used and stuck it into the dishwasher.

I made the call and wrote the note, and we were on our way.

As I'd guessed, Stephen (who's seven, like Joey) was happy to see us. The three boys were soon playing happily with Stephen's new computer game while Stacey and I hung out and watched.

"They're cute kids," Stacey whispered to me.

I nodded. "I think they'll fit in here just fine," I said.

Just then, Joey stood up and ran to the window. "I thought I heard a car," he explained after he'd looked outside. "But I guess it wasn't Dad."

"Even if it was," I said, "he'd know where to find you."

That didn't seem to reassure Joey. He kept popping up to look out the window every few minutes, and soon Nate was doing the same.

Stacey and I exchanged glances. "What if we invite Stephen over to your house?" I suggested. Maybe the boys would feel more comfortable at home.

"No!" said Nate.

"We're not supposed to invite people over," explained Joey.

"Maybe next time, when you've had the chance to ask your parents first," I suggested. "Meanwhile, why don't you try to relax and enjoy yourselves today?"

That helped for about five minutes. Then Mrs. Stanton-Cha came home, and at the sound of her car in the driveway both boys jumped up like jack-in-the-boxes.

"I guess it's time we headed home," I told them. Obviously they weren't going to relax.

When we returned to the Nichollses', both boys still seemed jumpy. I saw Joey find the note I'd left. He crumpled it up and threw it out. Then he put the pen I'd used in precisely the same place I'd taken it from, near the phone. After that, he and Nate sat down at the kitchen table to wait for their parents' return.

Mrs. Nicholls was the first one home. She came into the kitchen looking tired, but her eyes lit up when she saw the boys. "Hi, sweeties," she said. "Did you have fun with Claudia?"

"I think they did," I said, rushing to confess. It was as if the boys' nervousness was contagious. "We went over to the Stanton-Chas', next door. My friend Stacey was there, sitting for Stephen. I hope that was all right."

Mrs. Nicholls didn't seem upset. "That sounds nice. Why don't you boys say good-bye to Claudia and then run along and do your work?" she suggested.

Once Nate and Joey had left the room, Mrs. Nicholls paid me. "Taking the boys next door is fine with me, as long as it was okay with their father," she said, giving me a questioning look.

"Actually," I said, "I didn't think to ask him."

I noticed that Mrs. Nicholls looked pale. She bit her lip. Then she smiled. "I'm sure it's fine," she said, as if she were trying to convince herself instead of me. "Anyway, what he doesn't know won't hurt anyone," she added under her breath.

What was that supposed to mean? I was about to ask, but the kitchen clock caught my eye. "Oh, my lord," I gasped. "I better run, or I'll be late for my meeting." I said good-bye and ran out the door. My first job with the Nicholls boys had gone well, except for the slightly uneasy feeling I had as I left their house.

For the next couple of days, I forgot about the Nichollses. I have to admit I didn't think once about Joey or Nate. Why? Because I was too busy playing with Lynn. Every day after school I would race to the library. My mom was taking Lynn to work with her each day, where one of the assistants in the children's room was glad to keep an eye on her. I would run to find Lynn, then wrap her up in her quilted pink baby-bag. I'd carry her outside and pop her into her stroller. We'd wave bye-bye to my mom (I had to help Lynn with that) and head on home.

I'd prop Lynn in her infant seat while I had a snack, then carry her up to my room and spend the rest of the afternoon snuggling and playing with her on the bed. My baby cousin, a box of Junior Mints, and a Nancy Drew mystery I was reading for the fourth time: I was in heaven. Homework could wait for later, when my parents and Janine insisted on having their turns with Lynn. By Wednesday, when my friends arrived for the BSC meeting, I'd made a lot of progress teaching Lynn to say my name.

"Show them how you say my name," I told Lynn when everybody was there. "Say 'Claudia.' "

"K-K-gug," Lynn sputtered.

"See?" I said proudly.

"She said 'Gug,' " Kristy pointed out.

"So? That's how she says my name. She's only a baby, you know."

Kristy opened her mouth to answer, and that's when the phone rang. It was Mrs. Nicholls, calling to ask, first, if I could be Joey and Nate's regular sitter, and second, if I was free for a job the following afternoon. I said yes to both, after checking with the other members of the BSC. That's when I started thinking about Nate and Joey. I remembered how uncomfortable they'd seemed while playing at Stephen's, so I decided to bring my Kid-Kit the next day and see if they'd have a better time playing at home.

The next afternoon, Mr. Nicholls answered the door again when I arrived. He was wearing the same blue suit, and he left as quickly as he had before — after giving the boys the same lecture about behaving.

"I brought something special to show you

guys today," I told Joey and Nate once we were alone.

"Is it a puppy?" asked Nate.

I laughed. "Uh, no," I said.

"He really wants a puppy," Joey explained.

"I would take good care of it and always be nice to it," Nate said eagerly.

"Well, maybe someday you'll have a puppy," I said. Joey and Nate both looked doubtful. "Anyway," I went on, "what I brought today isn't a puppy. It's this." I brought my Kid-Kit out from behind my back. "Ta-da!" I said. The boys looked at the box, which I had just finished redecorating with pictures cut out from a nature magazine. The best one was of a charging elephant.

"What is it?" asked Joey.

"Are there lions inside?" Nate asked, edging away from the box.

"Nope," I said, opening it up. "Just toys. And books. And games and stickers and markers and all kinds of good stuff."

"Excellent!" cried Joey. "Can we see it all?"

"Definitely." We were in the living room, and I poured the contents of the box onto the rug, which made Joey look nervous. "Don't worry," I said. "We'll clean it all up before your parents come home. I just wanted you to see everything."

At that, Joey and Nate seemed to forget their

worries. They started going through the pile, exclaiming over each "find."

"Check it out!" cried Nate, holding up a Star Wars figure. "It's See-Threepio."

"Can I read this?" asked Joey, picking out an old Encyclopedia Brown book.

The boys had a blast going through my Kid-Kit. Finally, we settled down to play a game of checkers, me against both boys. Joey was a good player, and before long the boys' team was way ahead. Then Nate started whispering to Joey — I could have sworn he said something like "Better let her win" — and soon after that the game turned around and I ended up with about eight "kings" in five minutes.

After I won, the boys rummaged through the books and games again. Nate picked up a dog-eared, ancient copy of *The Runaway Bunny* and began to look through the pages, while Joey chose some markers. "Do you have any paper?" I asked him.

"There's some in the desk over there," he said, "but I'm not sure — "

"It's just paper," I said, interrupting him. "Nobody's going to be upset if we take one piece." We went to the desk together, and Joey showed me which drawer to open. I pulled out a sheet of plain paper, noticing that Joey was busy rearranging a small bowl of paper clips I'd nudged out of place. He put it back in its original spot, very carefully. I realized that Mr. Nicholls must like a tidy desk as much as he liked a tidy kitchen.

"Oh, no!" Nate suddenly cried. "I'm sorry, I'm sorry!"

"What is it?" I asked, rushing to him to see what was wrong.

He looked up at me and I saw fear in his eyes. "I — I tore your book," he said, showing me a page with a tiny tear in it. "I'll buy you a new one as soon as I can save up my allowance, I promise. Please, I'm really sorry."

He truly seemed to think I'd be furious with him for making a small tear in an old book. I reached out to pat his shoulder, and he jerked back. "Nate," I said, pulling my hand away and speaking as gently as I could. "It's really all right. That book is so old it would be hard *not* to tear the pages while you read it. I am not mad at all."

What was going on here? Had the boys had some terrible experience with a baby-sitter? Or was it me? Maybe I had done something to upset them. I watched the boys as they returned — carefully — to reading and drawing. I couldn't figure out what was making them so nervous.

"How about a snack?" I asked finally. "Are you two hungry?"

Nate nodded. So did Joey. They followed me

into the kitchen. I opened the cupboard over the fridge and began to pull down boxes.

"Not those crackers," said Joey. "We're not allowed to have those."

"We can't have those cookies either," Nate said, pointing to a bag. "Those are for Dad."

"Okay," I said. "How about some fruit?" A bowl full of apples, pears, and oranges was on the counter.

"That's for after dinner," Joey said. "But we could have some carrots or celery."

Finally I'd found something they could eat. But celery didn't sound too exciting. Unless — "Do you have any peanut butter?" I asked.

Nate pointed to another cabinet next to the fridge. "It's in there," he said.

"And is it okay to use some?" I asked.

The boys looked at each other. Then they nodded. "I think it's okay," said Joey.

"Great," I said. I found a knife and began spreading peanut butter onto celery sticks. Just as I'd finished the first one, the doorbell rang. I put down the knife, wiped my hands on a paper towel, and ran for the door with Joey and Nate trailing behind me.

I opened the door to find Mr. Nicholls standing there, looking a little sheepish. "I forgot my keys," he explained. He came in and looked the boys over. "Have you been good this afternoon?" he asked.

Joey and Nate nodded. Mr. Nicholls looked at me, and I found myself nodding too. "They're always good," I said.

"That's what I like to hear," said Mr. Nicholls over his shoulder as he headed for the kitchen. He was taking off his suit jacket and loosening his tie as he walked.

The boys and I went into the living room to put the toys and things back into my Kid-Kit. I was just dropping the last of the markers into their box when I sensed someone in the doorway. I looked up to see Mr. Nicholls standing there, holding the jar of peanut butter. I'd forgotten about our snack. It had seemed more important to clean up the living room.

"Who left this open on the counter?" he asked in a very quiet voice.

For a second, nobody answered. "I said, who left the peanut butter open on the counter?" Now his voice was much louder.

The boys didn't answer. I saw them draw closer together. I was so surprised that I couldn't say a word.

"I'm going to ask one more time," said Mr. Nicholls. And then he began to shout. "WHO LEFT THE — "

"I did," I said quickly. "It was me. I'm sorry. I was making us a snack when the doorbell rang, and — "

"No problem," said Mr. Nicholls calmly.

"Please forgive me for hollering. I thought it was one of my dumb, slobby sons who did it."

I was shocked. I'd never heard a parent talk that way. But Nate and Joey didn't even seem to notice.

"Now, can I offer you a ride home?" asked Mr. Nicholls. He sounded relaxed, even friendly.

"Thanks, no," I said quickly. "I can walk. It's not far." I could not fathom the idea of being alone in a car with Mr. Nicholls just then.

On my way out, I remembered something. "Hey," I said to the boys and their father. "Tomorrow there's going to be a planning meeting for the St. Patrick's Day parade. I'll take you guys, if you'd like to come, and if it's okay. They'll meet lots of kids there," I pointed out.

"I suppose it's all right," said Mr. Nicholls. I could tell he was still trying to be nice. "As long as you promise to tell me if my boys misbehave."

"Sure," I said. I knew Joey and Nate would behave just fine. They were good kids. I glanced at them on my way out, and when I saw their faces I could tell they were sorry to see me leave. I knew then that they hadn't had a bad experience with a baby-sitter.

I wasn't the one they were afraid of.

Chapter 5

Friday

Mal, I sure hope your parents weren't counting on having a nice lawn this year.

I don't know what my dad's going to say. I'll make Nicky explain.

At least the whole Pike family is due for some good luck!

I'll need it, when my parents see the yard....

Since Mal and Jessi were going to be sitting for Mal's brothers and sisters on Friday afternoon, they offered to host the St. Patrick's Day planning session. By the end of the day the kids had finally agreed on a great idea for the parade, but the process hadn't exactly been smooth.

The Pikes' lawn may never be smooth again either.

The kids were pretty excited about St. Patrick's Day. Jessi sensed that the moment she arrived at the Pikes' with her sister, Becca (who's eight), and Becca's friend Charlotte Johanssen (also eight).

"Top o' the mornin' to you!" yelled Adam, one of the ten-year-old Pike triplets, when Becca and Charlotte entered the yard. It was one of those warm, springlike days early March can bring. The grass was just beginning to turn green, little sprouts of tulip leaves were starting to push up in the flower garden, and a lone robin patrolled near the apple tree.

"It's not morning, silly," answered Charlotte.

"Top o' the afternoon, then," called Byron, another triplet.

The third triplet, Jordan, was hanging upside down by his knees from a branch of a nearby tree. "*Bottom* o' the afternoon," he shouted, cracking himself up. "Get it? Because I'm upside down?"

Becca and Charlotte exchanged a Look, rolling their eyes. They may be younger than the Pike triplets, but, as Becca once pointed out to Jessi, "girls mature faster than boys."

Claire and Margo, Mal's youngest sisters (Claire is five, Margo's seven), were busy playing "I Spy" — with an Irish twist. Everything they described had to be green *and* something else.

"I Spy with my little eye," chanted Margo, "something green and fuzzy."

Claire looked around. Then her eye lit upon Jessi. "Jessi's sweater!" she yelled. "My turn." She looked around again. "I Spy with my little eye . . . something green and slimy!"

"Boogers!" cried Nicky, her eight-year-old brother.

"Ew," said Margo.

"Nicky!" yelled Claire, stamping her foot. "You're not even playing. And anyway, I don't see any boogers."

"I do," said Nicky with a wicked grin. "They're hanging out of your nose." Laughing, he ran off before Claire could catch him.

"What did you see, anyway?" asked Margo curiously.

"A frog," said Claire, pointing. "That plastic one we lost last fall. I guess it isn't slimy, but a real frog would be."

Vanessa wandered over and picked up the frog. "I wonder if this frog is Irish," she said. "Can you imagine him dancing a jig?" She paused to think. "A pig doing a jig would rhyme better," she mused. "Maybe the frog should be dancing a *jog*."

Vanessa wants to be a poet when she's older. (She's nine now.) She spends a lot of time thinking up rhymes.

Mal and Jessi were sitting on the porch, watching all of this, when Kristy showed up with her stepsister, Karen (she's seven); her stepbrother, Andrew (four); and her brother David Michael, who's seven like Karen. The kids scattered to play with their friends, and Kristy plopped down next to Mal and Jessi.

"How's the planning going?" she asked.

Mal and Jessi looked at each other. "Oops," Mal replied.

Jessi smacked herself on the forehead. "I knew there was something we forgot!"

Kristy folded her arms and frowned. She was about to say something when Mal and Jessi started laughing.

"Just kidding," said Mal. "We thought we'd let the kids hang out for a bit first."

Kristy relaxed. "Good idea," she said. She stretched and yawned. "This sun feels great."

The three of them sat and chatted for awhile

until the sounds of arguing interrupted their peace.

"You faker," Nicky was yelling.

"It's not real," shouted Claire. "No fair!"

"You don't win the race," said Becca. "Cheater, cheater," she began to chant.

"What's going on?" Mal asked.

Adam, who was the one everyone was yelling at, answered, "We were having a contest to see who could find the first four-leaf clover because it's like a shamrock and it's Irish. Plus, it's lucky."

"Uh-huh," Mal said. She knew there must be more.

"And I found one," said Adam. "See?" he held up his fist.

Mal leaned close to look. "It sure looks like one," she said.

"Make him hand it over," cried Margo.

Mal held out her hand. Reluctantly, Adam gave her the "shamrock." It fell apart in Mal's hand. "It's two clovers you were holding together," she said. "The others are right."

Adam hung his head. "I was just playing."

"I know," said Mal gently. "No big deal." Then she looked around. "Oh, my lord," she cried. "This *is* a big deal. What did you guys do to this lawn?" She could see dozens of bare patches where the kids had been pulling up clumps of grass in their hurry to win the contest. "What a mess!" she wailed. "We have to fix this up."

"How about later?" called Kristy. I'd just arrived with Nate and Joey, and Kristy had decided it was time to start planning.

Mal took one last look at the lawn, sighed, and agreed. "How about if we all sit on the grass over here?" she asked.

Kristy, Jessi, and I helped round up all the kids. As we were organizing them into a circle, I heard Nate say to Joey, "Better not sit on the grass. You might stain your pants."

Joey nodded. "Okay. I'll sit on that stone," he said, pointing to a flat rock. "You can sit on your jacket because it's dark. Stains won't show."

Ordinarily, I would have told my charges not to worry. Now, after I'd seen Mr. Nicholls blow up over an open jar of peanut butter, I wasn't so sure. The boys were probably right to be careful. But it made me sad.

"Okay," said Kristy, after she'd whistled for everyone's attention. "Some of you have mentioned wanting to march in the St. Patrick's Day parade that Stoneybrook is sponsoring this year. Any ideas about what we could do that would be special and fun?"

Andrew, who was sitting between Joey and me, said something I couldn't quite hear.

"Speak up, dummy! Nobody can hear you," said Joey.

Andrew looked as if he were about to burst into tears.

I was shocked. I hadn't heard Joey talk that way before. I could see that my friends were surprised too. "Joey, calling names can hurt people's feelings," I said. "You could ask him nicely."

Joey looked ashamed. "I didn't mean — " he began. "Sorry," he said to Andrew. "I just wanted to make sure everyone could hear your idea." He looked at me as if to ask if that was better. I nodded.

"What was it, Andrew?" asked Kristy.

"I said I wanted us to have a marching band with big hats," he said. Everyone cracked up.

"I know what he means," Kristy said. "We went to the St. Patrick's Day parade in New York City once, and Andrew loved those guys in the big, tall, furry hats. They play bagpipes."

"We could do that!" cried Margo.

Kristy rolled her eyes. She *hates* bagpipes.

"I don't know," said Mal. "I think it might be pretty hard to learn to play bagpipes by St. Patrick's Day."

Kristy shot Mal a grateful look.

"Well, how about just the marching part?" asked Becca. "We could learn to do a march together."

"What if we dance instead of march?" asked

Karen. "I remember those dancing girls in the parade." She stood up and did an imitation of an Irish dancer, feet moving quickly and arms held straight down by her sides.

"Hey, that's great!" said Joey, sounding more like the boy I knew. He stood up and started dancing too.

"Irish dancing," mused Jessi. "That sounds like a great parade idea."

"But I was thinking of a float," I said. "Something with an Irish theme. And the kids could be dressed like leprechauns, and — "

"A float is too complicated," said Kristy. "You have to build it, and paint it, and everything."

"And paint is too messy," Nate agreed. I had a feeling he was worrying again about staining his clothes. "Let's just be dancers."

"Can we at least make costumes?" I asked. The dancing sounded good, but I wanted to be involved too, and I don't know much about dance.

Everyone agreed that costumes would be great, and we started thinking of ideas. Then, suddenly, Claire rolled over in the grass and gave a loud shriek.

"What is it?" asked Mal, rushing to her.

"I found one! I found one!" She was on her feet now, dancing around, holding something in her fist. Guess what it was?

A genuine four-leaf clover.

"Who's the bounciest baby," I sang as I walked around the kitchen with Lynn on my hip. "Who's the jounciest girl?"

Lynn giggled. She loves the little songs I make up for her.

I tested the formula I was heating. Nope, still too cold. I walked around some more. It was late Saturday afternoon, and before long I was going to have to leave Lynn in order to sit for the Nicholls boys. Now, I'd enjoyed sitting for the Nicholls boys, and I was looking forward to sitting for them again. But I didn't want to go just then. It meant giving up my last few hours with Lynn. While I was away, Peaches and Russ would come by to pick her up and take her home. "I hope your mommy and daddy had a great vacation," I told my cousin, rubbing noses with her. "I mean really *really* great, so they'll do it again soon!"

Lynn gurgled her agreement. She was such a happy baby.

I thought of Joey and Nate. Had they been happy babies too? Or had they always been nervous and shy? I had a feeling I knew the answer. Their personalities probably had a lot to do with the environment they'd grown up in. Mr. Nicholls was not exactly the sweet, loving, supportive type of parent I was used to. But I didn't want to judge him. I knew he was probably raising his kids the way he believed was right. Every parent has different ideas about how to bring up good kids.

"We're lucky, you and I," I told Lynn as I nuzzled her neck. I didn't remember my parents ever yelling at me or Janine the way Mr. Nicholls yelled at Joey and Nate. And I knew neither Russ nor Peaches would ever blow up at Lynn for doing something as minor as leaving a jar of peanut butter out on the counter.

I chatted with Lynn some more as I fed her a bottle and burped her. Then I changed her one last time and dressed her in the blue romper she looks so great in.

Finally, reluctantly, I gave her one more kiss and handed her over to my mom. It was time for me to leave for the Nichollses'.

"Well, hello, Claudia," said Mr. Nicholls, opening the door wide. I had to admit that he was always very nice to me. In fact, his friendliness made me doubt my memories of how stern he could be. Maybe I'd exaggerated his yelling and his strict rules.

"Honey, Claudia's here," he called up the stairs. Then he turned back to me. "You'll be giving the boys dinner," he said. "Everything's ready to stick into the microwave, and there's plenty for you as well."

He checked his watch, then looked up the stairs again, tapping his foot impatiently. "Let's move it, slowpoke," he yelled harshly. Then he grinned at me and shook his head. "Women," he said.

I didn't know what to say. After all, I am — or will be soon — a woman myself. And I didn't think it was very nice of him to speak to his wife that way, even if he was joking. But I didn't feel it was my place to challenge him, so I just gave him a weak smile in return.

Finally, Mrs. Nicholls appeared in a black dress and heels. "You look nice," I told her. She did, too. Her red lipstick was just right, and her hair was gleaming.

"She better look nice," said Mr. Nicholls. "It took her over an hour to pull herself together."

Mrs. Nicholls ignored him and smiled at me. "Thank you, Claudia," she said. "We won't be late tonight. Have a good time with the boys. I know they're looking forward to seeing you."

"Where are they?" I asked.

"In the living room, watching TV," answered Mr. Nicholls. "I told them to sit tight in there until you let them know dinner was ready."

I pictured the boys sitting stiffly on the sofa, hands folded in their laps, waiting obediently for dinner. With that image in mind, I hurried Mr. and Mrs. Nicholls out the door.

"Hi, guys," I called, poking my head into the living room. "Are you enjoying your show?" They looked almost exactly as I'd imagined, except that Joey was sitting on an easy chair and Nate was on the floor.

"Not really," admitted Nate. "It's kind of boring."

"Want to come help me make dinner?" I asked.

"Definitely!" said Joey, springing to his feet. "Dad never lets us help. He says we just get in the way. But I like to help when Mom lets us."

"Joey is a good cook too," Nate said. "You should see him mix cookie dough."

The boys followed me into the kitchen, and the three of us had dinner (microwave macaroni and cheese with steamed broccoli) on the table in no time flat. I poured milk for Joey, apple juice for Nate, and grape juice for me, and we sat down to eat.

"So, what did you guys do today?" I asked after a few quiet moments had passed.

Nate glanced up with a surprised look on his face. He didn't answer.

"Did you ride bikes? It was warm today. Or did you just hang out?"

Joey cleared his throat. "We — we aren't supposed to talk a lot during meals," he explained. "Like, it's okay to ask for the salt and stuff, but Dad says he likes quiet time to concentrate on his food."

I nodded. "Well, just for tonight, let's talk," I suggested. "I don't mind a little conversation while I eat." In fact, I was brought up to think that mealtime was family discussion time, but I didn't mention that.

The boys didn't need much encouragement. They relaxed, and talk flowed easily for the rest of the meal. I heard about their day in detail, along with news from the past week in school. Both of them seemed to have a lot to say.

Then I told them a little about Lynn. It was when I was showing them how I make her wave her arm that it happened.

I knocked over my grape juice.

Big deal, right? Well, apparently it was — in the Nicholls household.

Nate jumped up to grab the paper towels.

Joey jumped up to find the mop.

I tried to do my best with my napkin, but the juice ran all over the place.

"Now you're really going to get it," said

Joey, returning with the mop. At first I thought he must be joking, but when I looked at his face I realized he was serious.

"You're in big trouble," Nate agreed.

He was serious too. I still thought they were overreacting, but you know what? It was weird how worried I felt as I wiped at the mess until every trace of juice had disappeared. And how, for the rest of the evening, I found myself checking that my spill really was cleaned up.

After dinner we played cards for awhile (the boys let me win again) and before long it was time for bed. Now, bedtime can be a real struggle with some kids. But with Nate and Joey it was a breeze. For one thing, they were the ones who reminded me it was bedtime. For another, they jumped into their pajamas and brushed their teeth without having to be nagged. They even folded their clothes neatly before they hopped into the twin beds in their shared room.

Nate looked adorable with the covers pulled up to his chin. Adorable, but a little lonely. "Do you have a favorite stuffed animal that you like to take to bed?" I asked, looking around the room.

"We don't have any stuffed animals," Nate replied. "We're not allowed."

"Not allowed?" I repeated. How could a kid not be allowed to have stuffed animals?

"One time Mom bought us each one," he went on dreamily. He was already half asleep. "A tiger for me and a bear for Joey. But Dad said they were babyish, and he threw them away."

I drew in a quiet breath. Then I reached out to stroke Nate's soft, fine hair. He wasn't much more than a baby, really. He smiled up at me sleepily.

I smiled back, but my heart wasn't in it. Then I turned to Joey. He didn't look sleepy at all.

"Do you want me to read to you for awhile?" I asked.

He shook his head. "Bed is for sleeping," he said. It sounded like another of Mr. Nicholls's rules.

"But you don't look too sleepy," I answered.

"I'm not," he admitted. "But Claudia? If my dad asks, tell him that we both went to sleep right away, okay?"

I looked down at his anxious face. "Sure, Joey," I said. I pulled the covers up around his chin. "Good night, then. I'll be right downstairs if you need me."

The next couple of hours were quiet ones. I turned on the TV, just so I could forget the nervous look in Joey's eyes. Something wasn't right in the Nicholls household, but what could I do about it? I hated to see two kids so unhappy, but if Mr. Nicholls had his rules, who was I to question them? It was his house. Joey and Nate were his sons.

Mr. and Mrs. Nicholls came back early. (When I heard the car, I ran into the kitchen to check on the grape juice spill one last time.) As he was paying me, Mr. Nicholls asked me a lot of questions about how the boys had behaved. I told him the truth, that they'd been very, very good and had gone to bed without any problems. I'm not sure he believed me, but he seemed too tired to argue.

Since it was after dark, Mrs. Nicholls insisted on driving me home. The ride is short, but the silence in the car made it seem long. I didn't know what to say to her, and she seemed to be in another world. Finally, I mentioned something about Joey and Nate being excited about the St. Patrick's Day parade plans. She didn't say much, though.

When she dropped me off, she suddenly seemed to notice me. "Thank you, Claudia," she said as I unbuckled my seat belt. "And please tell your mother I said hello."

I promised that I would. In the dim glow of the streetlight, Mrs. Nicholls looked very sad. And I couldn't think of a single thing to say to cheer her up.

When I went inside that night, I said a quick good night to my parents and headed straight to my room. I needed to talk to someone about the Nichollses, and somehow I wasn't ready to tell my mom or dad about it. I called Stacey, and we spoke for a long time. Talking it over made me feel a little better, but I still felt confused about what to do.

At Monday's BSC meeting, I talked with the rest of my friends. I explained how much I liked Joey and Nate and how upsetting it was to see the way Mr. Nicholls treated them. We agreed that there wasn't much I could or should do about the situation. After all, while I didn't like Mr. Nicholls, it wasn't as if he were doing anything illegal. And when I told them that I wouldn't want Joey and Nate to feel as if I'd abandoned them, we agreed that I should continue sitting for them as long as I didn't feel too uncomfortable around Mr. Nicholls.

That sounded good to me, especially since I knew I wouldn't see much of him for the next few days. Joey and Nate and I would be out of the house, working on the St. Patrick's Day preparations.

Or so I thought.

I had a sitting job at the Nichollses' the following afternoon. Mr. Nicholls answered the door, just the way he always does. He was dressed in a suit again, so I assumed he was going on another job interview. He greeted me as pleasantly as always.

But something felt wrong. The house was too quiet, and Mr. Nicholls's smile seemed fake.

"Um, are the boys around?" I asked. "I was planning to take them over to my friend's house, to work on the St. Patrick's D —"

Mr. Nicholls cut me off. "They won't be going," he said flatly.

"But it's —"

"No buts," he said, dropping the fake smile entirely. "My sons have misbehaved, and they understand what that means. No going out. No TV. No snack. They'll be doing some housework this afternoon, and I'll need you to supervise."

"Uh, okay. What should they do?"

"They know," he said. "Just make sure they stick with it." He glanced at his watch. "I'll be back in a couple of hours." (In a couple of hours it will be close to 6:00, too late to go.) The fake smile returned. "Have a nice afternoon, Claudia," he said. "And just because the boys can't have a snack doesn't mean you have to go hungry. Help yourself."

Right. I wouldn't go near his kitchen, even if it was stuffed to the brim with Chee•tos and Cracker Jacks. I was beginning to realize that I just plain didn't like Mr. Nicholls.

But I did like his sons. I called to them as soon as their father had left. "Hey, Joey! Hey, Nate!" I said, trying to sound cheerful as I entered their room.

Both boys looked up briefly, but they didn't smile or meet my eyes. "Hi, Claudia," said Joey. Nate didn't say anything. Then they continued tidying up their room. Nate was dusting, swiping a rag over the contents of a bookcase on the far wall. Joey was rearranging a row of shoes in their shared closet. They worked quietly, as if what they were doing required all their attention.

"Hey, this room is looking terrific!" I said, still hoping for a smile.

Joey shrugged.

"Dad will find something wrong," Nate said. He balled up the rag as if he'd like to throw it away. Then he shook it out and started dusting again.

Obviously, nothing I could say was going to cheer the boys up. I might as well pitch in and help. "You know," I said, "I'm a whiz at cleaning windows."

"Uh-huh," said Joey, who was now concentrating on arranging the pencils on his desk.

"I'd be glad to do yours."

"Nate, run and find a bucket and some paper towels," Joey told his brother.

Nate left the room.

"It's not his fault," said Joey as soon as we were alone. "It's mine, but he's being punished too."

"What did you do?" I asked. It was hard to imagine Joey being bad enough to deserve such punishment.

"I touched Dad's briefcase," he said.

"You mean you took something from it?"

"No, I touched it," he repeated. "I was moving it out of the way of the racetrack we were building for our cars."

"Did you break it?" I asked. I was still confused.

"I told you," he said. "I touched it. That's against the rules. So we're being punished."

Whoa. So the boys had to stay inside all day to clean house, just because one of them had laid a finger on a briefcase. I shook my head and began to say something, but then I stopped. Maybe it was better if Joey didn't hear my opinion on the matter.

Nate returned with my window-cleaning supplies then. "Hey, all right!" I said. "Now we can do some real cleaning." I brushed off my hands and pushed up my sleeves, grinning.

For the next couple of hours, I acted like a peppy Ms. Clean, leading the boys around the house and cleaning every surface we could touch with a rag, brush, broom, or mop. Being busy took my mind off things. I hoped it did the same for the boys.

We finished up by organizing the recycling bins in the garage. I tried to make a game out of it, and for a few minutes the boys seemed distracted and almost happy.

Then Mr. Nicholls came home.

We heard the front door slam. Joey and Nate exchanged a frightened glance.

"Joey? Nate? Where are you? What's this mop doing out in the hall?" Mr. Nicholls sounded mad.

"I'll talk to him," I said quickly. "You guys finish up in here." I ran to the kitchen and found Mr. Nicholls shoving the mop back into the small closet we'd taken it from. From the look on his face, I had a feeling the job interview hadn't gone well.

"We left it out to dry," I said, trying to explain.

He turned, scowling. When he saw me, he tried to turn on that fake smile, but I could tell it took a big effort. "Where are the boys?" he asked.

"They're finishing up in the garage," I said. "They've been very, very good today." He snorted and began to walk toward the door to the garage. "Can I show you what we did?" I asked.

"Tell you what," he said, shoving his hand into his pocket. He pulled out a crumpled wad of bills, separated a few, and shoved them into my hand. "You're off duty. Bye-bye, now!"

I stood there for a second. Then I realized that if he wanted me to leave, I had to leave. On my way out, I remembered I'd left my jacket in the boys' room. I dashed upstairs to grab it.

Just as I reached the top step, jacket in hand, I heard Mr. Nicholls start to yell. "Where's my newspaper?" he roared. Then I heard the door to the garage fly open. "What did you little jerks do with my paper?"

"It — it might be in with the recycling," Joey answered, in such a tiny voice I could barely hear him.

Then I heard something louder, something that made my heart stop.

It was like the sound of a fish hitting the water.

It was like the sound of a stick hitting a drum.

It was like — no, it *was* — the sound of a hand hitting a face.

For a second, my knees felt so weak I thought I was going to fall down.

"What's it doing in there?" Mr. Nicholls shouted.

I wondered if I was going to hear another slap. I felt paralyzed. I felt like throwing up. I felt like running away.

But I couldn't leave those boys.

I tiptoed back down the stairs, almost too frightened to breathe. As I rounded the corner into the kitchen, Mr. Nicholls spotted me. "Hey, Claudia," he said casually. He flashed me that smile. "I didn't know you were still here."

Duh. If he'd known I was still there, would he have done what I thought he had done?

He angled his body as if to hide Joey and Nate, who stood behind him. It didn't work. I could see them both clearly, and I could see that they were crying. They didn't make a sound, but tears were rolling down their cheeks. And — I'm not one hundred percent positive about this — it looked to me as if Joey's right cheek was redder than his left.

"Do you need a ride home?" asked Mr. Nicholls. "I'd be glad to drive you."

"No." That's all I could squeak out. Not "No, thanks." Not "No, I can walk." Just "No."

I ran all the way home, with the picture of Joey's tear-stained face and Nate's brimming eyes haunting my mind.

The house was empty when I arrived. I ran straight to my room, grabbed the phone, and started dialing. It was time for an emergency meeting of the BSC.

Kristy wasn't home. Nobody answered at Abby's house.

Jessi wasn't home.

Mary Anne and Stacey were both out.

Finally, just as I was frantically dialing Mal's number, I remembered where everybody was. I ran back downstairs and out the door.

Tuesday

Well, we learned something today. Never attempt any kind of art project if Claudia isn't around to supervise! Once we saw that she wasn't coming, we should have just waited. Oh, well, the kids had fun. And that's the main thing, right?

Kristy wrote that entry in the BSC notebook toward the end of that afternoon's job at Mal's house. Or, to be more exact, in Mal's yard. With over a dozen kids. Fortunately, the other BSC members (except me) were on hand to help.

The plan? To make costumes for the St. Patrick's Day parade.

The materials? Lots of cardboard, plenty of paint (mostly green).

The scene? Total chaos.

The results? Hmmm . . . how can I put this nicely? Let's just say that if I had been there, things might have turned out differently.

The original bunch of kids — the Pikes, Becca and Charlotte, Karen, Andrew, and David Michael — had been joined by the Arnold twins, eight-year-old Marilyn and Carolyn, as well as by the Rodowsky boys: Shea (nine), Jackie (seven), and Archie (four). Jackie, otherwise known (to the BSC, in private) as the Walking Disaster, was holding the Rodowsky dog, Bo, on a long leash made of shoelaces.

"Mom says it's okay for us to bring Bo if it's okay with you," Jackie explained to Kristy sheepishly. "I even put on a leash I made from . . ." His eyes traveled down to his shoes, which were flopping around loosely. Shea's shoes looked the same, and Archie was tripping over his own feet. Jackie looked up at Kristy and grinned.

Kristy sighed and called to Mal, "Okay if Bo stays out here?"

"Sure," Mal said. "Pow's sleeping inside, so he won't mind." Pow is the Pikes' basset hound, and he's a lazy old dog. "We can tie Bo to this tree," she said, showing Jackie, "so he won't be in our way."

Jackie ran to his mom's car to tell her it was all right. (Kristy wasn't sure Mrs. Rodowsky knew about the "leash," but she figured she'd let it pass.) When Jackie returned, he knelt to tie up Bo. Then he ran to join the other kids, who by that time were clustered around the three folding tables Kristy and Mal had brought outside and covered with newspaper earlier. The tables were set up in a U shape, and each was supplied with jars of paint, big brushes, and a huge pile of cardboard.

"Where's Claudia?" Mary Anne asked.

Kristy shrugged. "Maybe she's not going to make it. I guess we don't have to wait for her. If we don't start soon, the kids are going to stage a mutiny."

"How hard can it be to make a few cardboard shamrocks?" asked Mal. The idea we'd come up with was to make cardboard cutouts that the kids could wear, sandwich-board-style, as they danced and marched their way down the street. Kristy thought a bunch of oversized shamrocks would look very cute.

"I don't want to make a shamrock," cried Margo. "I'm going to make a leprechaun."

"Uh-oh," said Jessi under her breath. "Does anybody know how to draw a leprechaun?"

"I do," said Mal, who draws very well. "But I'm going to be busy setting up paints. You guys can handle it."

"Sure!" said Kristy cheerfully. "It's just a little person with a top hat and pointed shoes." She was drawing on Margo's piece of cardboard as she spoke. "See?" She held it up.

"That looks more like a pterodactyl," said Byron.

"A sick pterodactyl," added Jordan.

"A pterodactyl with a p-tummy-ache," said Adam, laughing. "Get it? You spell tummy with a 'p' before the 't.' "

"Speaking of 'p,' " Abby said to Mal, "Archie just told me he has to use the bathroom. Okay if I take him inside?"

"Sure," said Mal. "Just don't let Pow out. If he realizes that Bo is out here in his yard, he might be mad."

Abby gave Mal the "okay" sign, took Archie by the hand, and led him into the house.

Meanwhile, Mary Anne was helping Vanessa draw a harp to cut out. "My teacher says the harp is an Irish symbol," said Vanessa. "It's sort of poetic, don't you think? I bet the ancient bards used to carry them."

While Vanessa was chatting, Mary Anne was drawing and erasing, drawing and erasing. "I thought I knew how to draw a harp," she finally said to Kristy. "But I'm beginning to wonder. Is this how it goes?" She held up the cardboard.

Kristy took one look and cracked up. "Another pterodactyl," she said. "Glad I'm not the only one around here who can't draw." Mary Anne looked hurt for a second. Then she cracked up too.

Claire, meanwhile, was working hard on her own piece of cardboard. Tongue between her teeth, she labored carefully, ignoring everyone else as she concentrated. On her way to help Marilyn and Carolyn cut out their twin shamrocks, Stacey glanced at Claire's drawing. "Very nice, Claire," she commented. "But — um — what is it?"

"An eye!" Claire pronounced proudly.

"An eye?"

Claire nodded. "See, here's the middle part, and here's the eyelashes, and here's the eyebrow —"

"I see, I see," said Stacey. "But why are you drawing an eye?"

"Because we're supposed to," said Claire. "Mal said we're making Irish things."

Stacey looked confused. Then she smiled. "Now I understand," she told Claire. "Here, let me show you something." She grabbed a piece of paper. "This is how 'eye' is spelled," she said patiently, writing out the word in capital letters. "And this is how you spell 'Irish.' The two words sound alike, but they're very different. 'Irish' means from Ireland." She was trying to be gentle with the news, since Claire is sensitive and can throw an excellent tantrum when she wants to.

But Claire just nodded. "Okay," she said cheerfully.

"You could make a shamrock," Stacey suggested, "or a leprechaun hat." (We'd decided by then that hats would be a lot easier than entire leprechauns.)

"That's okay," said Claire. "I like my eye. I'm going to finish it anyway, even if it isn't Irish." She picked up her pencil again and added another eyelash.

At that, Stacey shrugged and gave up, moving on to help the twins.

Over at the other table, Jessi and Mal were already opening paint for Shea, Andrew, and David Michael. "All set already?" asked Kristy, cruising by. "What did you guys decide to make?" She glanced over Jessi's shoulder. "Nice," she commented. "Nice — uh — shape."

"You don't know what it is, do you?" asked Mal.

"We'll give you a hint," said Jessi. "It's a rock."

"A rock?" Kristy guessed.

"A big Irish one," Mal said, grinning.

Kristy still looked confused.

"Ready, guys?" asked Jessi, coaching the three kids. "Let's tell Kristy what it is. All together, one, two, three —"

"The Blarney Stone!" they chorused.

Kristy cracked up. "That's great!" she said. "Good choice," she whispered to Jessi. "You thought of something easy to draw."

By then, almost all the kids had finished drawing and cutting out their Irish symbols.

"Keep a close eye on Jackie," Kristy whispered to Abby (who'd returned from the house). "Now that he's ready to paint, you can bet he'll find a way to make a mess."

Jackie's a terrific kid, but he does have a habit of making messes and breaking things, including his own bones. (That's why we call him the Walking Disaster.) He can't help it. He's just accident-prone.

"No problem," Abby whispered back. "He's on his way to the bathroom. He won't be anywhere near the paint for awhile."

Kristy nodded. "Great. Did you remind him not to let Pow out?"

Abby gulped. "Oops," she said.

Just then, Pow came galumphing out of the back door, barking his head off. Bo jumped up, instantly breaking the shoelace leash, and took off, with Pow behind him. The dogs raced around the yard, taking turns chasing each other.

"Catch them!" yelled Kristy.

Every last kid jumped up and began to run after the dogs. "Oh, no." Mary Anne groaned.

"Cover the paint!" Kristy called to Mal, who was still standing near the table. "Before the dogs —"

"Ohhhh," moaned everyone at once. Pow had just run headlong into the first table, spilling three jars of green paint onto Bo, who was behind him.

Jackie had done it again.

It took at least half an hour to clean up and start over again. This time, Bo was tied up more securely, with a clothesline "borrowed" from between two trees. He was still green, since Kristy figured the poster paint wouldn't hurt him. His bath could wait until later.

By the time I arrived, panting, most of the work was done and the kids were cleaning up for the second time.

"What do you think?" Kristy asked proudly, gesturing at a row of drying cardboard figures.

I didn't even glance at them. "We have to

have an emergency meeting!" I blurted out.

"Now?" asked Kristy, studying my face.

I nodded. Kristy must have seen how serious I was. "We'll meet you at your house in" — she glanced at her watch — "fifteen minutes," she said. "As soon as we make sure these kids are all home safely."

A safe home. Every other kid in that yard had one. But Nate and Joey didn't. What were we going to do about it?

I sat on my bed, waiting for everyone else to arrive. My mind was spinning. I looked around my room at all the familiar objects: the art on the walls, my overstuffed bookshelf, my collection of sea glass found on the beach. I felt so comfortable here, so sure of my place in the world. How would it feel to be Nate or Joey or any of the thousands of kids who couldn't feel secure in their own homes?

I couldn't imagine.

I didn't want to imagine.

But I knew I would never forget the sound of that slap, or the image of those two little boys standing behind their father, afraid of him.

I felt tears spring to my eyes, thinking of Nate and Joey, always worried about keeping things "just so." What kind of childhood was that?

I jumped when Kristy burst into my room. I'd been so caught up in my thoughts that I hadn't even heard her come up the stairs. "What happened?" she demanded.

"I heard —" I started to tell her, but then I thought better of it. I didn't want to have to repeat the horrible story more than I had to. "Let's wait until everyone's here," I said.

Kristy, who's not usually known as Ms. Sensitive, put a hand on my shoulder. "We'll help you work it out, whatever it is," she said softly.

I nearly began crying. Instead, trying to control my feelings, I said, "Have a Milky Way while you wait," and shoved a bag full of miniature chocolate bars into her hands.

Within a few minutes, all the other BSC members were on hand. Stacey and Mary Anne joined me on the bed, one on each side. Jessi, Mal, and Abby sprawled on the floor. Everyone looked at me expectantly. But I couldn't seem to speak the words I had to say.

"What is it, Claud?" asked Mary Anne gently after a few silent moments had passed.

"I heard — I think Mr. Nicholls — he hit one of the boys!" I blurted out. "And I don't mean a little spank."

"What?" Everyone gasped at once.

"Oh, no." Mary Anne put her hand over her mouth. "It can't be."

"Sure it can," said Kristy grimly. "Do you know how many abused children there are in this country?" She shook her head in disgust.

"I did a report on it for social studies last fall. It's unbelievable."

"But in Stoneybrook?" asked Mal.

"Everywhere," Kristy answered. "Rich people, poor people, people of all colors, shapes, and sizes hurt their kids." She turned back to me. "Tell us exactly what happened," she said. "Every detail. It's important."

I began my story with my arrival at the Nichollses' house that afternoon. I threw in a couple of things I hadn't had a chance to tell my friends before, such as the way the kids became so upset when I spilled my juice.

Then I explained why the boys hadn't been allowed to come to the St. Patrick's Day preparations.

"Because Joey did *what*?" asked Abby. "He *touched* his father's briefcase. Since when is that a crime?"

I shook my head. "Mr. Nicholls has a lot of rules," I said. "Now I know why the boys are so careful about following them."

"It's so awful," said Mary Anne.

"I know," I answered. "I thought his rules and his yelling were bad enough. But this —"

"Explain 'this,' " Kristy said. "We need to hear the rest."

So I told them about Mr. Nicholls coming home, and how he seemed to be in a terrible mood. "He was still acting nice to me," I said, remembering his fake smile, "but I was already starting to worry about the boys. I had a feeling he was going to yell at them no matter what they did." I paused. "But he did more than just yell." I told them the rest of the story. How Mr. Nicholls had paid me and told me to leave. How I'd gone upstairs to find my jacket. How he'd started yelling about his paper.

"Then I heard this sound," I said. "A slap."

"You heard it?" asked Kristy. "You didn't see anything?"

"No, I was still upstairs. But when I went down, the boys were crying and one of Joey's cheeks looked red."

"And Mr. Nicholls?" Kristy asked. "How did he act when he saw that you were still there?" She was gripping a ruler she'd taken from my desk. Her knuckles were white.

"He acted just the way he always acts around me," I said. "Like he's just this nice, regular guy. He offered me a ride home."

"Did you take it?" asked Jessi, her eyes wide.

"No way! I ran home, and that's when I realized you were all over at Mal's."

Everybody in the room looked stunned.

"We've never dealt with anything like this before," said Stacey. "What are we going to do?"

"That's a good question," said Kristy quietly. She was still gripping the ruler. "Accusing someone of child abuse is a big deal." She frowned. "But if it's true . . ."

"I think it is," I said. "I really do." I didn't know what else to say.

"But you didn't actually see anything," said Stacey. "Right? I mean, he could have — I'm not saying he did, but he could have — smacked the table to make that sound. All we know for sure is that Mr. Nicholls yells a lot. Plus, some parents *do* spank their children."

"His kids are totally afraid of him," added Abby.

"But these things aren't crimes," said Mal.

I understood why my friends were being so cautious. As Kristy said, child abuse is a very serious accusation. But none of my friends had seen Mr. Nicholls in action. I knew that I, for one, couldn't sit back and wait to see what happened next. I was about to say so when Kristy spoke up.

"Still," she said. "We have to do something. Even if we can't prove that he hits them. We have to tell someone."

Thank you, Kristy. "I agree," I said. "I know there's no way I'd go back there to sit unless we tell someone what's going on."

Jessi nodded. "Okay," she said. "But who do we tell? The police? A social worker?"

I gulped, imagining myself talking to someone official, someone who would question all my observations.

"Maybe you could start out by telling your mom," Abby suggested. "After all, she knows Mrs. Nicholls."

Mrs. Nicholls. I hadn't even thought of her. She must know what her husband was doing. Why didn't she stop him? Then I had a horrible thought. Maybe he treated her the same way. And maybe she was just as afraid of him as her sons were. "Ohhh." I sighed, holding my head in my hands. This was way more than I could deal with. "I think I do need to talk to my mom," I said.

"Or you could talk to mine," suggested Kristy. "She's great in an emergency."

"My dad might be able to give us some legal advice," put in Mary Anne.

"Thanks, guys," I said. "But I think I really want to talk to my own mom. And soon."

"Do you want us to be there while you do it?" asked Kristy. "You can do the talking, but we'll be here, just for support."

I looked around the room at my friends. "That would be great," I answered.

Just then, I heard the front door open downstairs. "I bet that's her now," I said. "I'll go see."

I headed downstairs and found my mom in

the kitchen, putting a kettle of water on the stove for tea. She almost always has a cup after work.

"Mom, can you come upstairs? We're having a special BSC meeting, and we wanted to talk to you about something."

"Sure, honey," she said. She was leafing through a stack of mail, so I don't think she saw my face. If she had, she'd have known how upset I was. "I'll be up as soon as my tea's ready."

"Thanks," I said. Back upstairs, my friends and I waited quietly until there was a tap on the door.

"Hi, Mrs. Kishi," said Mary Anne.

"Hello, Mary Anne. Hello, everyone. What's up? Are you looking for book recommendations for your charges? Or is this about the fund-raiser next month? I knew you'd have some good ideas for that."

"Do you want to sit down?" asked Kristy, jumping up to offer her the director's chair.

My mom thanked Kristy. She sat down and put her cup of tea on my desk. Then she looked at me, really *looked* at me. "This is serious, isn't it?" she asked. She reached over to take my hand. "Go on, Claudia," she said. "Tell me."

I told the entire story again. Mom listened closely, holding my hand. Watching her face, I saw that while she was as upset as the rest of us, she was not exactly surprised. Maybe she'd sensed something from the way Mrs. Nicholls behaved. Or maybe it was just that, working at the library, she'd learned enough about the subject of child abuse to know it could happen anywhere. Maybe she'd even heard of other cases in Stoneybrook.

Her first concern was for me, though. "Are you okay, sweetie?" she asked. "That must have been so upsetting. And scary."

Once again, I almost started to cry. Instead, I gulped back my tears. It wasn't that I was embarrassed to cry in front of my friends. They would understand. It was just that I wanted to move forward, figure out what we were going to do next.

So I nodded. "I'm okay. But I'm really worried about Joey and Nate. What can we do to help them?"

"You've taken the first big step, which was to come to me," said my mom. "And I'm really glad you did. I know it couldn't have been easy to figure out how to handle this."

We all shook our heads.

"And it's not going to be much easier for awhile," said Mom. "Child abuse is an extremely serious accusation. Even health care professionals have to be very careful about how they handle cases that come into the emergency room or a doctor's office. Still, they are almost always required to report the cases to the authorities — even if they only suspect the children are at risk and don't have solid proof. Right now, we're in that gray area — we have a suspicion of risk, but no real evidence."

"Claudia's not making up what she saw and heard," said Abby.

"I'm not saying she is. I know my daughter, and I know she wouldn't lie about a thing like this. But she did not see Mr. Nicholls hit his child."

"We all think he probably did, though," said Kristy. "From what we've seen. Remember, guys, how Joey spoke to Andrew that day over at Mal's? I bet he was copying the way his dad acts."

"And I remember how nervous the boys

were about grass stains and things," added Mal. "I know a lot of boys, and none of them gives a second thought to things like that."

Stacey told Mom how I'd called her when I first started sitting for the Nichollses. "Claudia knew something was wrong from the start," she said.

My mother nodded. "I believe you," she said. "But I need to take some time to think about what to do next. I want to talk to a friend of mine who is a social worker. Plus, I want to talk to Mrs. Nicholls."

"I know you'll figure something out, Mrs. Kishi," said Kristy. "Claud, are you okay now? I have to go home for dinner."

"I'm okay," I said. "Thanks, everybody. We'll talk some more tomorrow."

My friends left after we agreed to keep things quiet until Mom decided what to do. My mother stayed behind. She sat next to me on the bed. "Oh, Claudia," she said, rubbing my back. "I'm so sorry. Sometimes I wish I could protect you from all the awful things in the world, the way I could when you were just a baby. But I can't, can I?"

I shook my head. "I guess not," I said, thinking once more of the way Nate and Joey had looked the last time I'd seen them. The person who was supposed to be protecting them was hurting them instead.

That's when I started to cry. Mom held me as I sobbed and sobbed.

It's funny. I used to feel closer to Mimi, my grandmother, than to my mom. I could talk to Mimi about anything, and I knew she understood me best. I've missed that closeness more than anyone can imagine. But at that moment, in my room, I felt closer to my mom than I had in a long, long time.

"Mom," I finally asked, once my tears subsided, "why does it happen? How could somebody hit a kid?"

"Oh, Claudia," she said, "it's so complicated. Usually, though, if a person hurts someone else it's because *he's* hurting. Lots of people who hurt their kids were abused themselves when they were younger."

"What about Mrs. Nicholls?" I asked. "Why does she stay with him? How could she let him hurt the boys?"

"That's even more complicated. It's hard to understand, but I'll tell you one thing for sure. Even though I haven't known her long, I know her well enough to say that she loves the boys. And seeing them hurt is probably torture for her. But for some reason she feels powerless and doesn't know how to make Mr. Nicholls stop."

"So what happens next?" I asked, sniffling a little.

"I don't know. I'm going to have to give it a lot of thought." She stood up and moved to my desk. "But first I want to make some notes about what you've told me, so I can be sure I have a clear idea of what you've seen and heard."

I gave her a notebook and a pen and stood beside her as she wrote down what I'd told her, adding dates and times in case the notes were ever needed by the authorities. Fortunately, she remembered everything, and I didn't have to go through the story again.

When she finished, Mom and I went downstairs to fix dinner. Afterward she and my dad talked for a long time in the study. I tried to concentrate on my homework, but it didn't seem very important. (Figuring out what *x* equals *never* feels especially meaningful to me, but that night it seemed more pointless than ever.)

Finally, at about nine-thirty, Mom tapped on my door and came in. "I've discussed things with your dad," she told me, "and with the social worker I know through the library. We all agree that a good first step would be for me to talk with Mrs. Nicholls."

I nodded. "Okay," I said. I felt relieved to know that my mother was taking charge. Whatever she decided was fine, as long as *something* was done. If it were up to me, I would have put Mr. Nicholls behind bars that very night. But I knew that wasn't how things worked. And it wouldn't be right, anyway, since I couldn't prove anything.

As I went to sleep that night, I thought once more about Nate and Joey. Only this time, I tried not to picture their tear-stained faces. I tried to imagine them happy and secure. I saw Nate holding a big, soft stuffed tiger as he slipped off to sleep, cozy in a warm, safe bed. And I pictured Joey at an easel, joyfully painting a beautiful picture with every color of paint in his paintbox, not caring for a second about messing up his clothes.

Trying to concentrate on my homework that night was nothing compared to trying to concentrate in school the next day.

I moved through the halls on automatic pilot, following the wave of students as they went from class to class. And, while I was supposed to be listening to a lecture on *Johnny Tremain*, or on the way a bill becomes a law, or on why we should care about how fast some train would travel if it went ten miles per hour faster than some other train — while I was supposed to be listening to all that, I wasn't. I was thinking about Nate and Joey and Mr. Nicholls and — most of all — Mrs. Nicholls, and whether or not my mom had talked to her yet.

I kept checking the clock and thinking, *She must have told her by now.* Or, *Maybe they're talking about it right this minute*. The school day had never seemed longer.

Finally, the last bell rang and I was free to

run home. The first thing I did was check the answering machine. Maybe Mom had left a message for me.

The machine was blinking, but when I pushed PLAY all I heard was a message about some meeting my dad was supposed to attend that night. Disappointed, I wandered into the kitchen to fix myself a snack.

One microwaved burrito later, I was still a nervous wreck. How long was I going to have to wait to find out what had happened?

My eye strayed toward the phone on the kitchen wall. Should I call and find out for myself instead of waiting? Why not? I picked up the phone, dialed, and listened to one ring before I slammed the receiver back into its cradle. What if Mrs. Nicholls answered the phone? What would I say? Would she recognize my voice?

I played around with a few fake accents, wondering if I could fool her if I sounded French or British. Then I realized I was just being silly. Chances were she wouldn't even answer the phone. I tried to remember exactly what her job was at the library. My mom had said something about filing — that's all I knew. I pictured Mrs. Nicholls and my mom standing next to a big filing cabinet, talking.

I tried to imagine how the conversation would go.

I knew my mom would be gentle and considerate, and that she would start off slowly, maybe by asking Mrs. Nicholls how the kids were adjusting to their new home.

"Oh, fine," Mrs. Nicholls would say.

"And do they like having Claudia as a sitter?"

"They adore her."

"She's very fond of them as well." Mom would pause. "That's why she's a little concerned about their well-being," she would add. "She's noticed that Mr. Nicholls has a bit of a temper. . . ."

Mrs. Nicholls would blush and look at the floor. "He's testy because he's out of work," she'd say. "Sometimes he yells."

Mom would nod. "But I have the feeling he may be doing more than just yelling at the boys," she'd say carefully.

At that point, Mrs. Nicholls would break down and cry. Then she'd beg my mother to help her figure out what to do. And together they'd make a plan.

Which would be — what? I didn't have the slightest idea. How did people deal with a situation like this? Maybe they'd make Mr. Nicholls promise never to do it again. Maybe he'd have to go to counseling. In any case, I knew things would start to change for the better as soon as Mom and Mrs. Nicholls talked.

But had they talked yet or not? I glanced at the clock. It was only four. I had at least two hours to go if I waited until Mom came home.

I grabbed the phone and dialed again. This time I let it ring twice before I hung up. *What a chicken,* I told myself. I decided just to wait until my mother came home.

Upstairs in my room, I spent some time reorganizing my junk food stash. I moved a bag of Chips Ahoy from my sock drawer into one of the shoe compartments in my closet. I transferred a package of Oreos from my right-hand desk drawer to the one on the left. And I reburied a bag of Sour Patch Kids in a place I refuse to tell anyone about. A girl has to have *some* secrets.

That job done, I turned to my homework. Algebra, naturally, was far less attention-grabbing than junk food, and I found my mind drifting again, making up another conversation between Mom and Mrs. Nicholls. In this one, Mrs. Nicholls confessed everything before Mom even had a chance to air her suspicions. And she told Mom that she was already working things out with a social worker who was going to help Mr. Nicholls overcome his problem. Meanwhile, the boys would be sent to stay with their aunt, whom they adored.

That was a good one. *See?* I told myself. *There are a lot of ways this could work out fine.*

I'd only made it through one set of math problems when I heard the door open and close downstairs. Was that her? Maybe she was home early. I ran to the top of the stairs. "Mom?" I called.

"No, it is I, Janine," answered my grammatically correct sister. "But I'm only dashing in for a second. I have an evening class tonight." I heard her rummaging around in the kitchen and decided not to bother her. She sounded busy and rushed.

I went back to my math homework and struggled through another set of problems. I had a feeling I was putting down a lot of wrong answers, but at least I was trying. If I was lucky, my math teacher would appreciate the effort.

I had floated into a fantasy in which Mrs. Nicholls asks my mom if we would be willing to take care of Joey and Nate for awhile when, once again, I heard the door open and shut downstairs. This time it was my mom, and she came straight to my room. She didn't even pause to make herself a cup of tea.

She did not look happy. In fact, I hadn't seen her look so upset in a long time. Before she even said anything, I knew that her talk with Mrs. Nicholls had not been a success. It certainly hadn't followed any of the story lines *I'd* come up with.

She sat down on the bed and patted the place next to her. I settled in. "So?" I asked.

She sighed. "It didn't go well, Claudia," she said.

"What happened?"

"Well, I approached Mrs. Nicholls first thing in the morning, when nobody else was in the office. I was careful about what I said, because I didn't want to make her feel defensive. But she did anyway."

"What did she do?"

"She denied everything," my mother said, sounding tired.

"You mean she acted as if Mr. Nicholls never yelled at the kids, or made those ridiculous rules, or hit them, or anything?" I couldn't believe my ears.

"That's right. She said he was a good father. The only thing she would admit is that he's 'a little strict.' Other than that, she clammed up."

I groaned.

"But there was something about her," my mother continued, "that made me positive she wasn't telling the truth. She wouldn't meet my eyes. Her answers sounded rehearsed. And, I don't think she knew it, but she was wringing her hands the whole time."

"So what did you do?" I asked.

"What could I do? I didn't want to make her even more upset. So I eased off. After our talk, she avoided me for the rest of the day — or tried to, anyway. Every time I saw her, I attempted to say a few words about how she really should talk to someone, and that if she didn't want to talk to me there were other people who would listen. I even slipped her the name and number of the social worker."

I shook my head. "I just hope she talks to someone soon," I said. "What can we do while we're waiting?"

"I don't know. I think we've done the right thing, but it doesn't seem like enough. I'm going to have to call the Department of Children and Youth Services. Mona — my friend who's a social worker — knows someone there. They will be able to look into this case in a thorough, professional way. Really, it's beyond us now." She looked confused, which was exactly how I felt.

Just then, my phone rang. I didn't feel like talking to anyone, but since mine is the official BSC number I had to answer. "Hello?" I said.

"Claudia, it's me." I recognized Kristy's voice.

"What's up?"

"The weirdest thing just happened. Mrs. Nicholls called me. I had to tell you about it right now, instead of waiting for our meeting."

"What?" I cried. "Why did she call you?"

"I guess she knew my name because I'm listed as president on our fliers. And she must have seen my number on the fliers."

"But what did she say?"

"She canceled all of her BSC appointments. Every one."

Oh, no. I couldn't think of a thing to say to Kristy, so we just said good-bye and hung up. I told Mom what had happened.

She shook her head. "I hope I'm doing the right thing," she said, as if she were talking to herself.

I hoped so too.

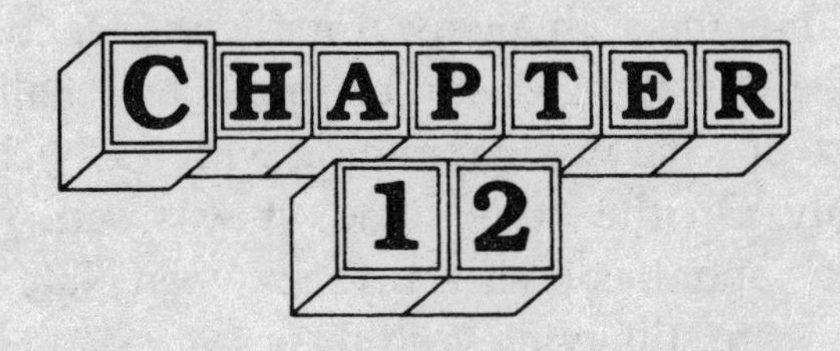

Saturday

At first, I didn't think I'd be able to enjoy the parade. We're all upset about the Nichollses. But you know what? I managed to have a really good time. And so did the kids. I guess it's just another reminder that life goes on....

I liked reading Abby's notes about helping with the St. Patrick's Day parade. I ended up having a decent time too, and so did the other BSC members. In a way, it made me feel better to see that things hadn't ground to a halt because of what was happening with the Nicholls family. On the other hand, it was sad. I felt guilty about enjoying myself when Nate and Joey were still living with their scary dad.

I hadn't seen either of the boys since Tuesday. Mom said that Mrs. Nicholls was still avoiding her at work. Mom and I talked every day about what to do next, and my friends and I had chewed over the subject in our BSC meetings too. But so far, the only thing we could do was wait. I still had some hope that Mrs. Nicholls would come to her senses and talk to someone.

Meanwhile, the BSC was also caught up in final preparations for the St. Patrick's Day parade. Kristy had asked Abby to coordinate our group, so the rest of us took orders from her. She'd told us to show up at Brenner Field at eight on Saturday morning. "That's the staging area," she'd explained, "where all the groups in the parade will meet and get organized."

From there, the parade was going to wind its way to Main Street, through downtown Stoneybrook, and return by way of Rosedale

Road and Burnt Hill Road. Our group was to be smack in the middle of the parade, according to Abby, who was in touch with the parade organizers. In front of us would be the marching band, and in back of us would be a float from Bloomer's nursery.

Abby had assigned each of us a job. Mine was to oversee the kids' costumes. That meant arriving early to 1) make sure each kid had remembered to bring a costume and 2) help with adjustments or problems.

I struggled out of bed at seven (not an easy job for me since I like to sleep in on weekends) and made it to Brenner Field by five after eight. I was working on excuses for being late, but when I arrived I discovered they were unnecessary. The only other people on hand were BSC members. Nobody else in the whole parade had arrived yet!

"Abby, what time is the parade supposed to start?" I asked.

She blushed. "Not until ten," she answered. "I just wanted to make sure we were ready."

As it turned out, the extra time came in handy when the kids began to arrive minutes later. Charlotte was so excited about the parade that she had forgotten her costume. Marilyn Arnold had ripped hers. And Nicky Pike had spilled maple syrup ("We had pancakes for breakfast," he explained) down the front of his.

The rest of the kids needed help tying on their costumes. Each of the kids wore two big pieces of cardboard, front and back, with straps over their shoulders holding the costume up, and ties holding it together at the sides. And several of the paint jobs needed touching up.

I was working on Claire's giant eye costume when I noticed Abby nearby, talking to a woman in a long green dress. "That's Maggie O'Meara," Kristy whispered to me. "She used to live in Stoneybrook. She's a famous Irish singer."

"Cool," I said. "What's she doing in an evening gown?"

"She's the grand marshal of the parade," Kristy told me, just as Maggie O'Meara walked toward us.

"The grandmother?" asked Claire, who'd overheard. "Why does a parade need a grandmother?"

"I said grand *marshal*. It means she's the one who leads the parade," explained Kristy.

Maggie O'Meara had heard the exchange, and she was smiling. "Good morning, lassies," she said. "And how are you on this lovely day?" She had a soft, lilting accent.

"It's not lovely, it's yucky," said Claire.

She was right. None of us had wanted to dwell on it, but the weather wasn't terrific for a parade. It wasn't cold, but the skies were gray and I'd felt an occasional drizzle as I went about my work.

"Yucky?" asked Maggie O'Meara with a smile. "In the old country, we'd call this a soft day. After all, it's not pouring, is it? And the winds aren't howling."

"And the weather report says it'll be nicer later on," added Abby, who'd joined us.

Maggie O'Meara nodded. "With a bit of luck, the sun will shine on us. In any case, I just wanted to welcome you to our parade. Let's see your costume, lassie," she said to Claire. Claire stood up proudly and turned slowly, showing off her eye. I cringed a little, expecting Maggie O'Meara to laugh, or ask what an eye had to do with St. Patrick's Day. Instead, she said, "Clever girl," then sang, " 'When Irish eyes are smiling'!"

As Maggie O'Meara left, Claire let out a whoop. "She liked my costume best!"

"Only because she didn't see mine," said Byron, showing off his leprechaun-hat costume.

Just then, Archie Rodowsky wandered by, crying quietly. "Archie?" asked Abby. "What's the matter?"

"N-N-Nobody knows what I'm supposed to be," he said, sniffling.

Abby stood back to take a look at his lumpy gray costume.

I joined her. "What *is* he supposed to be?" I

whispered into her ear. Since I'd missed the costume-making day, I had no idea.

"The Blarney Stone," she whispered back.

"That's great!"

"I know. But if nobody understands, he'll be upset all day." She turned to Archie. "Tell you what," she said. "I'm going to make you a little sign, okay? Then everybody will know what you are."

Once the other kids saw Archie's sign, everybody wanted one. Most of the shapes were strange enough to need explanations, anyway.

"This wouldn't have happened if you'd been around the day we made the costumes, Claud," Abby said to me as she pinned an I AM A SHAMROCK sign onto Margo's costume.

Suddenly, a siren sounded. "That's the ten-minute warning," Abby called. "Are we almost ready? Gather around so we can see."

Soon our entire contingent was assembled. Weird shapes or not, the kids looked pretty cute. And when Stacey turned on the tape player she'd brought and they tried out some dance moves to the Irish music, I thought they looked terrific. Especially when the sun broke through the clouds and the day turned into the lovely one Maggie O'Meara had predicted.

By then, the field was full of paraders. There were three marching bands, two groups of bagpipers, and a drum corps, all of whom were warming up by playing at top volume. Police officers on horses roamed the field.

Several businesses had sponsored floats. Bloomer's nursery had covered theirs with green plants and had put little leprechaun statues behind them, so that they peeped out at the audience. A "rainbow" made of crepe paper fluttered over the scene.

"Look at the Polly's Fine Candy Float!" called Nicky. "I wish we were marching behind them."

The candy store had sponsored a float with clowns in green costumes. Each clown carried a huge basket of candy, which he or she would toss to the crowd by the handful.

"That other float is boring," pointed out Charlotte.

I had to agree. Several beauty shops from Stoneybrook and neighboring towns had grouped together to sponsor a float featuring Miss Teenage Stoneybrook, Little Miss Connecticut, and a bunch of other pageant winners. They weren't doing anything, as Charlotte had noticed. They just sat on their platforms, dressed in their perfect, princess-y dresses, ready to wave at their adoring public. I had a feeling the clowns would be much more popular.

The siren sounded again, and Abby shooed us into place. It was time to march. The kids stepped out proudly, and we baby-sitters marched alongside, trying to look inconspicuous as we kept an eye on our charges.

I scanned the crowd as we marched through downtown Stoneybrook, hoping to catch sight of Joey or Nate if they happened to be at the parade. A few of the kids had asked where they were, and I'd explained that they had other plans and couldn't march. I'd been hoping that those "other plans" I'd invented included watching the parade. Unfortunately, that didn't seem to be the case. If they were there, I didn't spot them. And, even though I ended up enjoying the parade, I never did stop wondering how Joey and Nate were doing.

"Claudia? This is Erica Blumberg. I wanted to ask you something. Didn't you used to baby-sit for the Nicholls boys?"

I sat down on my bed, gripping the phone.

"Claudia?"

For just a second, I couldn't speak. Somehow, I knew that this call meant that something had happened to Joey and Nate. Erica is a level-headed, responsible girl I know from school. She wouldn't be calling unless something was really wrong.

It was the Tuesday after the parade. I still hadn't had any contact with the Nicholls boys. And Mrs. Nicholls was still avoiding my mother at work. *Especially* after the caseworker from the Department of Children and Youth Services called her. The only marginally good thing I'd heard was from Stacey, who'd seen Joey and Nate at Stoneybrook Elementary when she picked up Charlotte from school on

Monday afternoon. Stacey had said that the boys looked fine.

But now, Erica was calling me and a tone in her voice made me feel weak in the knees.

"Sure," I said, finally answering her. "I sat for them several times."

"That's what they told me. Anyway, I guess — um — well, I've sat for them three times." Erica's voice was hushed. "And I'm sitting for them today. The boys are up in their room. So I wanted to ask you — did you notice anything weird about this family?"

"Weird?" I echoed. My heart was thudding around in my chest. "Erica, has something happened?"

"I'm not sure," Erica said carefully. "I mean, the first time I baby-sat here I thought everything was fine. I thought they were just a normal family. But then I heard Mr. Nicholls yelling, and then today —" She broke off.

"What?" I asked. "What happened?" I knew my voice sounded panicky. I tried to calm down. I didn't want to frighten Erica.

"It's just that" — Erica lowered her voice so that I could barely hear her — "when I arrived, Mr. Nicholls told me that the boys were being punished, and that they were in their room. I was supposed to just stay downstairs and leave them alone. But after awhile, I heard crying from up there and I had to see what was wrong."

"And?" I asked.

"Claudia, when I saw them, I —"

"What?"

"Joey has a black eye. And Nate has some bruises on his arm." She said it all in one quick rush.

"Oh, my lord." I closed my eyes tight and drew in a breath.

"It may not be what we think," said Erica hurriedly. "When I asked the boys about it, Joey had a story about slipping on a skate-board and hitting his eye on the doorknob, and Nate told me he was hit in the arm by a softball at school yesterday. But Claudia, I don't believe them," she added quietly.

"I don't either," I said. My brain felt numb. Erica was calling me for help, but I had no idea what to tell her. Then I thought of my mom. "Erica, when is Mr. Nicholls due back?"

"I don't know." She sounded scared. "I think he's out on a job interview. He said he'd be back in a couple of hours."

"Okay, stay there with the boys. I'm going to call my mom. She'll know what to do."

"But —"

"Just do it, Erica," I said. "Try to stay calm around Joey and Nate." I hung up and punched in the number for the library. It seemed to take forever for someone to answer. Finally, a woman — not Mrs. Nicholls, fortunately — picked up the phone.

"Stoneybrook Public Library," she said.

"Mrs. Kishi, please," I said.

"I'm sorry, she's in a meeting. Can I have her call you back?"

"This is her daughter," I said. "It's an emergency. Could you please ask her to come to the phone?"

The woman said she'd try, and put me on hold. I sat waiting for what seemed like hours but was probably only seconds.

"Claudia?" My mother's voice was full of concern.

"Mom, you have to help. I think Joey and Nate are in trouble. Erica Blumberg is sitting for them, and she just called to say that Joey has a black eye and Nate has —"

My mom interrupted me. "I'll take care of it," she said. "I'm glad you called." She was all business now.

"What are you going to do?" I asked.

"I'm going to go get those boys out of that house," she said firmly. "I'll call you back as soon as I know anything."

"Can I — ?" I began, but my mom had already hung up.

I hung up too, and sat there for a few seconds, staring at the phone. Then I jumped up and started to pace around the room. I thought of Joey and Nate, trying too hard to hide the truth of what had happened. I thought of Erica, waiting with the boys. And I thought of my mom, racing toward them, determined to move them out of harm's way. And what about Mrs. Nicholls? Where was she? And — Mr. Nicholls? He could show up any minute. What would Erica do if he came home before my mom arrived?

I wondered if I should call Kristy, or any of my other BSC friends. But why? What could they possibly do to help?

I looked at the phone. How long would it be before I heard from my mom? How could I possibly stand to wait?

Finally, I realized I couldn't just wait. I ran down the stairs, grabbed my jacket, and flew out the door. My bike was leaning against the garage. I jumped onto it and started pedaling hard. *At least,* I thought, *I can be there to help Erica.*

It's not far to the Nichollses' house. I was there within ten minutes. And as I rode into sight of it, I saw my mom's car pull into the driveway. Then I saw her and Mrs. Nicholls climb out and rush into the house without a second glance at me. I realized that my mom must have told Mrs. Nicholls what had happened and brought her along. They must have left Mrs. Nicholls's car at the library.

Then I realized something else.

My mom's car was not the only one in the driveway.

Mr. Nicholls's car was there too, pulled up close to the garage. He'd come home!

Suddenly, I heard yelling inside, and then a horrible, crashing sound — the sound of something breaking. I was still holding my bike, but now I laid it on its side. I wasn't sure what to do. Should I run away? Maybe I should call the police. What was happening inside?

Without warning, the front door opened. My heart skipped a beat. Then I saw Joey and Nate standing there, with Erica close behind them. All three looked petrified. Joey and Nate looked young and scared and very, very vulnerable. "Go on," said Erica, giving the boys a gentle nudge.

"Joey!" I cried. I'd just caught sight of his injured eye, and my stomach flipped over. Joey looked up and saw me. He tried to smile. Nate gave me a tiny wave. "Come on, boys," I said, opening my arms.

They looked wary, but they walked toward me. "Are you okay?" I asked, smoothing Joey's hair back from his forehead. "Don't be scared," I added, hugging Nate. "We'll take care of you."

I glanced up at Erica, who had followed the boys. "What happened?" I mouthed.

"He came home," she answered quietly.

Just then the door opened again. This time, my mom and Mrs. Nicholls came out, walking backward as if they knew it wouldn't be safe to turn their backs on the open door. My mom looked over her shoulder and saw us on the lawn. "Get in the car," she said. "Everyone. Get in the car right now." Her voice was level, but I could tell she was working hard to control it.

I grabbed Joey's hand and Erica took Nate's. We ran toward my mom's car, pulling the boys along with us. Mom and Mrs. Nicholls had reached the car by then, and Mom had already hopped in and started the engine. I opened the door to the backseat and helped Joey and Nate in, then followed them. Erica went to the other side of the car to help fasten seat belts. I threw my bike in the trunk.

"Never mind the seat belts for now," said my mom. (I never, in a million years, thought I'd hear her say those words.) "Everybody in?"

She turned to count heads. And at that moment, I heard the front door slam. My heart thudded crazily in my chest until I saw the empty porch and realized that Mr. Nicholls had closed the door from inside.

"I guess he's not coming out," Mrs. Nicholls

said in a flat voice. "He's going to let us go." I couldn't tell what she was feeling. Relief? Fear? Sadness?

My mom didn't answer. Instead, she patted Mrs. Nicholls on the shoulder. Then she put the car into reverse and backed down the driveway.

And as we drove away down Elm Street, I let out a huge sigh, almost a sob. I felt as if I'd been holding my breath for a million years.

"Is everybody okay?" my mother asked. Her eyes met mine in the rearview mirror. "We're safe now. Let's all just take a big, deep breath and try to relax a little. And Claudia, you can check those seat belts now."

She sounded so steady and controlled. I don't know how she did it. I tried to do as she said and take a deep breath. Then I fixed the boys' belts. In the front seat, Mrs. Nicholls sat with her head in her hands, sobbing quietly. Erica and I exchanged a glance over Joey's and Nate's heads. Her eyes were still wide. Whatever she'd seen had really scared her. Nate sat next to me, tears running down his face. I had the feeling he didn't even know how hard he was clutching my hand. Joey sat on the other side of Nate, arms folded close to his chest. He wore a blank expression. I winced every time I glanced at him and saw that black eye.

"Erica, I'm going to drop you off at home, if

that's all right," my mom said. "Don't you live on Forest Drive?"

Erica nodded, then realized my mother couldn't hear a nod. "Yes," she said, barely squeaking out the word.

"Will somebody be home? Somebody you can talk to?" asked my mom. She sounded concerned.

Erica nodded again. "My mom's usually home by now."

"Good. We'll call you later to check in and see how you're doing."

"Okay." I could tell Erica was about to burst into tears, and I couldn't blame her.

When my mom pulled up in front of her house, Erica gave each of the boys a quick hug good-bye and thanked my mother. She whispered a good-bye to Mrs. Nicholls, who was still crying. Then she jumped out and ran to her house without looking back.

"Mom?" I asked as we drove away. "Where are we going?" I could tell she had some kind of plan in mind.

"To Stamford," my mother answered. "To your father's office. Nobody will think to look for us there, at least, not right away."

By "nobody," I knew she meant Mr. Nicholls.

Mrs. Nicholls raised her tear-stained face for a second to look at my mom. "Thank you," she choked out. "Thank you."

Nobody talked much on the way to Stamford. My mom concentrated on her driving. Nate finally stopped crying, but his mother couldn't seem to. Joey's face was still blank. And me? I was in a state of shock. Everything had happened so fast.

In Stamford, rush hour was beginning and the traffic was heavy. Slowly, we made our way to the building where my dad works, and my mom parked in an underground garage nearby. We climbed out of the car and stretched. Mom took me aside. "Let me go up first," she said. "I'll explain things to Dad."

We gave her a head start, waiting in the garage until Nate whispered to me that he had to "go." I checked my watch and figured that Mom had had a few minutes with my dad by then, so I led the way to his office, making a stop at the men's room. The office was emptying out by then, so we received only a few looks from employees as we trooped through the halls.

"Welcome," Dad said, opening the door to let us in. His face was serious, but his expression was warm. He showed Mrs. Nicholls to the small couch along one wall of his office (he's been known to nap on it, but don't tell his boss). Then he and Mom sat down facing her.

I took the boys to my dad's desk and tried to distract them quietly. I showed them how his chair spins around and let them try out all his pens. Then I remembered he has a tic-tac-toe game on his computer, and I set that up for them to play. By then Joey had begun to look less frozen, and Nate's tears had dried. They were still scared but I had the feeling they were beginning to feel a little relieved too. I was glad they knew me well enough to feel safe and comfortable with me.

Meanwhile, I kept one ear out for the conversation between my parents and Mrs. Nicholls. She couldn't stop thanking them, and she kept apologizing to my mom for avoiding her in the past week. "It's so hard to explain," she kept saying. "I know you can't understand it, but I do still love him. And I kept hoping that things would improve."

"We'll do our best to understand," said my mother. "We certainly don't judge you for wanting to keep your family together. But for now —"

"I know, I know," said Mrs. Nicholls. "For now, we just have to make sure the boys are safe. And that means I'm not going home. Not for awhile, and maybe not ever. I also need to call Ms. Barber from the Department of Children and Youth Services — I might even have to call . . . the police." She started crying all over again when she said that. My father handed her a box of tissues, and my mom made comforting sounds.

Then they moved on to the next question. "Have you thought about where to go?" asked my mother.

"Have I thought about it?" echoed Mrs. Nicholls. "I've thought about it all the time. I just kept hoping it wouldn't come to this." She sighed. "But now it has. So I think what I'll do is call my sister. She lives in upstate New York, about four hours from here. She's always begging me to bring the boys for a long visit."

"That sounds perfect," said my dad. "Would you like to use my phone to call her?"

Mrs. Nicholls nodded and blew her nose on a tissue.

While she made the call, my parents had a quick conversation. Then my mom said to me, "If you feel comfortable staying here with Mrs. Nicholls and the boys, your father and I will drive back to Stoneybrook to fetch her car. Then she can leave from here to go to New York."

I told her that was fine with me. I felt safe in my dad's office, and I could see that the boys did too. And spending a little time here would give everyone a chance to calm down and relax a bit. "Is that Chinese restaurant still across the street?" I asked. "Maybe I could call and order some food while we're waiting."

"Terrific idea," said Mom. She opened her purse and gave me some money. Then she squeezed my shoulder. "Thank you, Claudia," she whispered.

By then, Mrs. Nicholls had finished her call. "She says she can't wait to see us," she reported. "And guess what, boys? Aunt Sissy has a brand-new puppy. Won't that be fun?" She was still sniffing, but her tears had stopped for the moment.

My parents left, and the four of us pored over a menu from the Chinese restaurant. Then, over egg rolls and vegetable lo mein, we talked about puppies and car trips and games Mrs. Nicholls and her sister used to play when they were young. We talked about all kinds of things — except for the one *big* thing that none of us could stop thinking about. Then, just as we were polishing off the last of the fortune cookies, my parents returned.

"You have a full tank of gas," my father told Mrs. Nicholls, "and we've stocked the car with juice and snacks. I think you're all set."

"How can I thank you?" asked Mrs. Nicholls. "You've done so much, and I —"

"Shhh," said my mother. "Thanks aren't necessary. Just, please, take care of yourself. And let us know how you are. Call collect, anytime. Call soon."

Mrs. Nicholls hugged me and my parents.

Then I knelt and opened my arms for a big hug from Joey and Nate. "I'll miss you," I told them.

We walked them down to the parking garage, watched as they settled into their car, and waved as they drove away. Then we climbed into our own car, and my father started the engine. The second my mother closed the door behind her, she began to cry. I joined her, and it was a big relief to cry. After awhile, we began to talk about what had happened.

"I know it's hard," said my dad, reaching out to pat my mom's hand, "but I think they'll be better off."

"I sure hope so." My mom sighed.

"It can't be any worse," I added, thinking of the way Mr. Nicholls treated his sons. "At least they won't be in danger."

"But this isn't the end of the story," my father reminded me. "The Nichollses have to face this issue and deal with it. That may mean a divorce, or it might mean that Mr. Nicholls realizes he needs help and begins to deal with his problem. Mrs. Nicholls is going to call the woman from the Department of Children and Youth Services, and hopefully they'll find a way to work things out."

I nodded. I knew there was still a long way to go for the Nichollses. But I couldn't help being glad about the fact that Joey and Nate would be sleeping soundly and safely that night, far away from their father.

I didn't sleep too soundly myself that night. I tossed and turned, thinking I'd never fall asleep. And then, just when I felt myself drifting off, the phone rang. I checked the clock as I answered. It was midnight. Who could be calling?

"Hello?" I said sleepily.

There was a pause. Then I heard a man's voice, yelling so loudly that I had to hold the phone away from my ear. "Give me back my wife!" he shouted. Then he started to cry.

It was Mr. Nicholls.

I hung up without saying a word. And then I lay awake for the rest of the night.

Somehow, I made it through the next day. I think I was sleepwalking through most of my classes. After school I came home and, after a quick snack, lay down for what I thought would be a ten-minute nap.

I didn't wake up until Kristy burst into my room. "Time for our meeting, sleepyhead!" she said, tickling my feet.

I groaned. But then I sat up, rubbed my eyes, and started to think about what junk food I had hidden where. "Is Erica coming?" I asked. I'd suggested to Kristy that we invite Erica to our meeting. My mom told me about this thing called "closure," which means you've talked something over and worked it out, until you feel ready to move on. She was the one who suggested that we use our regular BSC meeting to try to reach some closure on what had just happened.

"I talked to her during science class, and she said she would," Kristy answered.

At lunchtime that day, I'd given my friends an update on what had happened the day before — from Erica's call to Mr. Nicholls's. I knew that by now someone would have told Mal and Jessi (who have a different lunch period) about it too. I was grateful for that. It meant I wouldn't have to tell the whole horrible story all over again.

I rummaged around under my bed and came up with a bag of peanut M&M's. Then I walked to my bookshelf, pulled out a dictionary, and checked behind it. Sure enough, there was a box of Triscuits. Good. I was prepared for company.

Stacey showed up next, and then Mary Anne arrived. By five-thirty, everyone was on hand, including Erica. I passed around the munchies and we began to talk about what had happened.

"I can't believe he called here last night," said Erica. She was sitting on the floor, near Jessi and Mal. She hugged her knees. "That's just so, so creepy."

"I know," I said. I helped myself to a small handful of Triscuits. "I hope that never happens again."

"If it does, we'll just have to change our business number," said Kristy.

That surprised me. I would have expected her to fight that idea to the bitter end. "What about our clients?" I asked. "They're all used to this number."

"They can learn a new one," said Kristy, shrugging. She popped two yellow M&M's into her mouth. "I'm more concerned about you getting enough sleep. The BSC needs you."

Hearing that felt good. I had to admit I was looking forward to sitting for some of our regular, uncomplicated clients. Even Jackie Rodowsky would be a breeze after what I'd been through.

"I still don't understand," said Jessi, musing. "How can anybody hit their kids? Kids are defenseless, and they look to adults for protection. How could he do it?"

"It's awful," I agreed. "It's the worst."

Erica nodded. She was the only other one who really knew how awful it was. She knew and liked Joey and Nate. And she'd seen their father in action. "My dad says there's a fund in Stoneybrook to help families who are in this kind of trouble. I'm going to send them all the money I earned when I was sitting for the Nichollses."

"What a great idea!" I said. "Will you give me their address? I'd like to send some too."

Erica promised to bring it to school the next day.

"I hope we never run into this problem again," said Abby, "but if we do, is there anything we should do differently?"

"I think we handled it really well," said Kristy. "But I think we should always tell an adult right away, as soon as we suspect something. We could have done that a little sooner."

We all nodded. "And if something serious happens, call somebody immediately — the way Erica called Claudia," said Stacey.

"Right," agreed Mary Anne. "Don't try to handle it on your own." She looked terrified just thinking about it.

"That's the real lesson here," I said. "I know I felt a whole lot better as soon as we told my mom. It was just too much for us to deal with by ourselves." Just then, I heard footsteps on the stairs. "Quick!" I said in a whisper. "Hide the candy!"

Kristy shoved the M&M's underneath a notebook on my desk. Abby tossed the box of Triscuits to Mary Anne, who slid it under my pillow. Then there was a light knock on my door. "Claudia?" asked my mother. "It's me. May I come in?"

Kristy jumped up to open the door. "Sure," she said. "You're always welcome."

Always — as long as I have time to hide the evidence!

Mom sat down on the director's chair, and

Kristy settled in on the floor. "I just wanted to give you an update on what's happening with the Nichollses," she began.

"Did you talk to Mrs. Nicholls?" I asked. "How are the boys?"

Mom smiled. "Nate and Joey are fine. And yes, I did talk to Mrs. Nicholls. She's feeling safe at her sister's house. She's still a little shaky, but I think she knows she did the right thing."

It was no surprise to hear that Mrs. Nicholls felt shaky. I still did. "What else?" I asked.

"She's spoken to the people from the Department of Children and Youth Services. The police have become involved — there's a restraining order on Mr. Nicholls, so he won't go near them. He's agreed to have counseling, which is a start."

"Did he admit anything?" asked Erica.

My mother nodded. She looked sad. "Yes, he did," she said. "Mrs. Nicholls said that he talked about wanting to work on his 'problem.' "

"That's great," said Stacey. "Isn't it?"

My mother shrugged. "It's great that he wants to change, but it may not be easy." She sighed. "I think he has a long way to go before he's ready to be a good father to those boys."

"But at least Joey and Nate are safe now," I said.

"Yes. And from what Mrs. Nicholls told me, their aunt's new puppy is the perfect distraction. That will help, for now. They are going to talk to a counselor too, to help sort things out. And I think Mrs. Nicholls may decide to settle near her sister and start the boys in school there."

"Wow," I said. "So they might not come back to Stoneybrook — ever."

Mom nodded.

So the boys were safe and sound. That was good. Who could have guessed that sitting for the Nicholls family would turn out to be the biggest challenge the BSC had ever faced? I knew we had handled it well and done the right thing. But I also knew that this wasn't exactly a happy ending. I wondered if I would ever see Joey and Nate again. No matter how their lives turned out, I hoped they would be happy.

That night, as I turned out the light and rolled over to go to sleep, I thought about the boys again. I made up my mind to go downtown to the toy store after school the next day. I'd buy a floppy tiger for Nate and a teddy bear for Joey. I liked picturing the boys sleeping peacefully and safely, stuffed toys cradled in their arms.

Dear Reader,

In *Claudia and the Terrible Truth*, Claudia learns a disturbing secret about a new family in Stoneybrook. When she thinks that Joey and Nate are being abused, she isn't sure what to do. What if she's wrong? Finally, though, Claudia decides she must talk to an adult. This is a good rule to follow for any serious baby-sitting problem. It's always better to be safe than sorry. Don't worry about bringing up an issue that turns out not to be a problem. Trust your instincts. Chances are, if you think something is wrong, it probably is. And the best thing to do is to talk to any adult you can trust. Claudia chose her mother. You might choose a parent, a teacher, a clergyperson, or your doctor.

For more information concerning child abuse, you or an adult can call:

Childhelp USA National Hotline
1-800-4-A-CHILD®

Happy reading,

Ann M Martin

L. GODWIN

Ann M. Martin

About the Author

Ann Matthews Martin was born on August 12, 1955. She grew up in Princeton, NJ, with her parents and her younger sister, Jane.

Although Ann used to be a teacher and then an editor of children's books, she's now a full-time writer. She gets ideas for her books from many different places. Some are based on personal experiences. Others are based on childhood memories and feelings. Many are written about contemporary problems or events.

All of Ann's characters, even the members of the Baby-sitters Club, are made up. (So is Stoneybrook.) But many of her characters are based on real people. Sometimes Ann names her characters after people she knows; other times she chooses names she likes.

In addition to the Baby-sitters Club books, Ann Martin has written many other books for children. Her favorite is *Ten Kids, No Pets* because she loves big families and she loves animals. Her favorite Baby-sitters Club book is *Kristy's Big Day.* (By the way, Kristy is her favorite baby-sitter!)

Ann M. Martin now lives in New York with her cats, Gussie and Woody. Her hobbies are reading, sewing, and needlework — especially making clothes for children.

Notebook Pages

This Baby-sitters Club book belongs to ______________________.

I am __________ years old and in the ______________________ grade.

The name of my school is ______________________________.

I got this BSC book from ______________________________.

I started reading it on ______________________________ and finished reading it on ______________________________.

The place where I read most of this book is ______________.

My favorite part was when ______________________________.

If I could change anything in the story, it might be the part when ____.

My favorite character in the Baby-sitters Club is ____________.

The BSC member I am most like is ______________________ because ____.

If I could write a Baby-sitters Club book it would be about ____ ____.

#117 Claudia and the Terrible Truth

In *Claudia and the Terrible Truth,* Claudia needs to figure out how to get help for Joey and Nate Nicholls. First she talks to her friends in the BSC. Then she realizes that she needs to talk to an adult. In a difficult situation, the friends I would talk to first are ____________ ____________ because ______________________________ ______________. If I needed to talk to an adult, I would talk to ______________________________. Another adult I trust is ________ ______________________________. As Claudia learns, it is very important to talk to someone when you think someone is in danger. If I had been in Claudia's situation, this is what I would have done: ______________________________

____

______________________________.

CLAUDIA'S

Finger painting at 3...

a spooky sitting adventu

Sitting for two of my favorite charges --
Jamie and Lucy Newton.

SCRAPBOOK

...oil painting
at 13!

my family. Mom and Dad, me and
Janine... and we'll never forget Mimi.

Interior art by Angelo Tillery

Read all the books
about **Claudia**
in the Baby-sitters Club series
by Ann M. Martin

#2 *Claudia and the Phantom Phone Calls*
Someone mysterious is calling Claudia!

#7 *Claudia and Mean Janine*
Claudia's big sister is super smart . . . and super mean.

#12 *Claudia and the New Girl*
Claudia might give up the club — and it's all Ashley's fault.

#19 *Claudia and the Bad Joke*
When Claudia baby-sits for a practical joker, she's headed for big trouble.

#26 *Claudia and the Sad Good-bye*
Claudia never thought anything bad would happen to her grandmother, Mimi.

#33 *Claudia and the Great Search*
Claudia thinks she was adopted — and no one told her about it.

#40 *Claudia and the Middle School Mystery*
How could anyone accuse *Claudia* of cheating?

#49 *Claudia and the Genius of Elm Street*
Baby-sitting for a seven-year-old genius makes Claudia feel like a world-class dunce.

#56 *Keep Out, Claudia!*
Who wouldn't want Claudia for a baby-sitter?

#63 *Claudia's ~~Freind~~ Friend*
Claudia and Shea can't spell — but they can be friends!

#71 *Claudia and the Perfect Boy*
Love is in the air when Claudia starts a personals column in the school paper.

#78 *Claudia and Crazy Peaches*
Claudia's crazy Aunt Peaches is back in town. Let the games begin!

#85 *Claudia Kishi, Live From WSTO!*
Claudia wins a contest to have her own radio show.

#91 *Claudia and the First Thanksgiving*
Claudia's in the middle of a big Thanksgiving controversy!

#97 *Claudia and the World's Cutest Baby*
Claudia can't take her eyes off her adorable new niece.

#101 *Claudia Kishi, Middle School Dropout*
It's back to seventh grade for Claudia . . . and she's *not* happy about it.

#106 *Claudia, Queen of the Seventh Grade*
When it comes to seventh grade, Claudia rules!

#113 *Claudia Makes Up Her Mind*
Boys . . . grades . . . Claudia has too many big choices to make.

#117 *Claudia and the Terrible Truth*
Something is horribly wrong at the Nicholls house.

Mysteries:

#6 *The Mystery at Claudia's House*
Claudia's room has been ransacked! Can the baby-sitters track down whodunnit?

#11 *Claudia and the Mystery at the Museum*
Burglaries, forgeries . . . something crooked is going on at the new museum in Stoneybrook!

#16 *Claudia and the Clue in the Photograph*
Has Claudia caught a thief — on film?

#21 *Claudia and the Recipe for Danger*
There's nothing half-baked about the attempts to sabotage a big cooking contest!

#27 *Claudia and the Lighthouse Ghost*
This ghost wants *revenge.*

Portrait Collection:

Claudia's Book
Claudia's design for living.

Look for #118

KRISTY THOMAS, DOG TRAINER

I couldn't help but think, the moment I saw Scout, that she was extra-special. She was a beautiful chocolate-colored Labrador retriever. I fell in love with her instantly.

We went through a training session and saw a video about guide dogs for the blind and how to be a good puppy walker. Then Gillian gave us the Foundation handbook with all the basic information on raising Scout. She went over it with us, patiently answering all our questions. Both Mom and Watson took careful notes.

Scout came with her own collar, special ID tags, and leash. We also got two bowls, a starter bag of the kind of dog food we were supposed to feed her, a crate for her to sleep in, and two Nylabones for her to chew. We were also given a yellow coat for her to wear that identified her as a guide dog puppy in training, so that she could be taken everywhere (just as she would be when she became a working guide dog for the blind). Oh yes, we got her medical records too, and forms we were supposed to fill out in order to keep track of her progress for the Guide Dog Foundation, with which we would be in touch at least once a month.

After Watson filled out some more forms, we put Scout in her crate (which was basically a big cage) and put her in the car. The whole time Scout looked a little anxious, but mostly she was calm. Karen and David Michael sat on either side of her.

Karen petted the kennel. "Don't worry, Scout," she said. "We're going to do everything just right. You're going to have the best puppy walker family in the whole wide world."

I really hoped she was right.

Collect and read these exciting BSC Super Specials, Mysteries, and Super Mysteries along with your favorite Baby-sitters Club books!

BSC Super Specials

❑ BBK44240-6	Baby-sitters on Board! Super Special #1	$3.95
❑ BBK44239-2	Baby-sitters' Summer Vacation Super Special #2	$3.95
❑ BBK43973-1	Baby-sitters' Winter Vacation Super Special #3	$3.95
❑ BBK42493-9	Baby-sitters' Island Adventure Super Special #4	$3.95
❑ BBK43575-2	California Girls! Super Special #5	$3.95
❑ BBK43576-0	New York, New York! Super Special #6	$4.50
❑ BBK44963-X	Snowbound! Super Special #7	$3.95
❑ BBK44962-X	Baby-sitters at Shadow Lake Super Special #8	$3.95
❑ BBK45661-X	Starring The Baby-sitters Club! Super Special #9	$3.95
❑ BBK45674-1	Sea City, Here We Come! Super Special #10	$3.95
❑ BBK47015-9	The Baby-sitters Remember Super Special #11	$3.95
❑ BBK48308-0	Here Come the Bridesmaids! Super Special #12	$3.95
❑ BBK22883-8	Aloha, Baby-sitters! Super Special #13	$4.50
❑ BBK69126-X	BSC in the USA Super Special #14	$4.50

BSC Mysteries

❑ BAI44084-5	#1 Stacey and the Missing Ring	$3.50
❑ BAI44085-3	#2 Beware Dawn!	$3.50
❑ BAI44799-8	#3 Mallory and the Ghost Cat	$3.50
❑ BAI44800-5	#4 Kristy and the Missing Child	$3.50
❑ BAI44801-3	#5 Mary Anne and the Secret in the Attic	$3.50
❑ BAI44961-3	#6 The Mystery at Claudia's House	$3.50
❑ BAI44960-5	#7 Dawn and the Disappearing Dogs	$3.50
❑ BAI44959-1	#8 Jessi and the Jewel Thieves	$3.50
❑ BAI44958-3	#9 Kristy and the Haunted Mansion	$3.50
❑ BAI45696-2	#10 Stacey and the Mystery Money	$3.50

More titles ➡

THE BABY-SITTERS CLUB®
FAN CLUB
Only $8.95!
Plus $2.00 Postage and Handling
Get all this great stuff!
❶ 110-mm camera!
❷ Mini photo album!
❸ Keepsake shipper!
❹ Poster!
❺ Diary!
❻ Note cards!
❼ Stickers!
❽ Eight pencils!
❾ Fan Club newsletter!*
Fan Club Friendship Pack
Secret Diary